Oldcat and Ms Puss

. . . Verily I say unto you, Except ye be converted, and become as little children, ye shall not enter into the kingdom of heaven.

Matthew 18:3

Lear: Yet you see how this world goes.
Gloucester: I see it feelingly.

King Lear, IV, 6

Oldcat and Ms Puss

A Book of Days for You and Me

By Joe Taylor

Black Belt Press
Montgomery

Black Belt Press
P.O. Box 551
Montgomery, AL 36101

Grateful acknowledgment to the following magazines, in which the following passages from this book appeared in slightly altered forms:
"Saturdays," in *The Chattahoochee Review* and *The Chattahoochee Review: Fifteenth Anniversary Year;* "Cold Sores, Body Odors, and Credit Cards," in *A Gathering of Tribes*; "Doing Own Thing" in *Cornfield Review*; "Number Four, Please" (now entitled "Norman Vincent's Peal") and "Sleepless Hollow," in *Yemassee*; "Feminist Deconstruction" and "Big Boat" in *Whiskey Island Magazine*

Thanks to Judy Thead for the title "Edifice Complex."
Much thanks to David Gosselin for his artwork.

Library of Congress Cataloging-in-Publication Data

Taylor, Joe, 1949-
Oldcat and Ms Puss : a book of days for you and me / by Joe Taylor.
p. cm.
ISBN 1-881320-72-3
I. Title.
PS3570.A9395043 1997
813'.54—dc21 97-438
CIP

Design by Randall Williams
Printed in the United States of America
97 98 99 5 4 3 2 1

The Black Belt, defined by its dark, rich soil, stretches across central Alabama. It was the heart of the cotton belt. It was and is a place of great beauty, of extreme wealth and grinding poverty, of pain and joy. Here we take our stand, listening to the past, looking to the future.

for Tricia,

and for Tom Abrams

Contents

Thursdays

Fridays

Saturdays

Sundays

Mondays

The Prickle-up Effect

The first job offered Oldcat after college come from Timely Electronics in Gainesville. Oldcat suspect he hired cause Timely president remember him from Florida's BIG GAME #8 against Florida State. Umhmm, oh yeah, Oldcat remember too: that game, early fourth quarter, was when him back receive its final relocation notice—with, so sorry, no moving expense allowed, just doctor bills forever.

Anyway, this sportball fan Mr Brown, President and Bossman Deluxe of Timely Electronics, he a misplaced blue-blood-red czar, dictatoring in wrong century, wrong country, wrong city. Still, he do pay American technicolor greenback; moresomeover, Oldcat never want to depart Gainesville, because he fancy himself in forever-love with U of Florida daffodil.

So job he take.

Three days after his first disappointing paycheck, this daffodil—who obviously change major to accounting—break date with humble him, a broke-back low-salaried ex-football star, to fine-dine lobster thermidor with Some Hero He, The Illustrious Gainesville Lawyer. That be capital T, capital I, capital G, capital L, thank you so very much, esquire.

But not all sadness and small letters. For after only three months, Oldcat receive promotion to supervisory position and think, *I come into my own now, show daffodil who a real man. Maybe I* **get** *job because of my funked sportball past, but not so for this promotion: it come because I a big capital H hit, thank you so very much, Esquire.*

Nearly true. Oldcat discover himself to be off by only several letters: instead of esquire, he a square; instead of hit, he a big capital S shit. The why of this? At Bossman Deluxe Brown's Timely Electronics plant, distance make soul grow fonder of Czar Brown, who still dictatoring like plant located in retrograd Petrograd. For instance: Czar Brown look jim-fine-dandy on paycheck's facsimile autograph; why, him even appear a jovial, bold-stroke fellow on initialed memorandums shortening lunch breaks and/or parking lot. But when in real-life spotting him at thirty feet, alert employees scamper toward exits, for at ten feet, spittle drool continual from him ever-babbling lip; at six feet, him gray eyes fuzz; and at two feet, him pincer claws grab. *Woe unto thee, blockaded myopic employee! To buy contact lens, you wait too late!*

"Do this, do that," babbling Bossman always order any close-by worker, his thin mouth gurgling underneath his twitched crab nose. "Say yessir, say nossir. Say smilesir when me smile, say laughsir when me laugh."

This treatment serf bad enough, but if Bossman Deluxe ever maneuver a supervisor alone, things groan worse, for then Bossman sure to detail private, intricate, long-pondered, ingenious theory of math: "All we need do, young man, is change America over to the Babylonian system of base thirteen and Joe and Jill Taxpayer will save a cool 400 million green simoleons the first year alone because the Babylonian system works *that* much more efficient than our Arabic decimal system of base ten. Ha. Credit those A-rabs—trying to screw us over even then! Speaking of screw, tell me true, son: did the coaches at U of F really let you football types gang-bang those foxy cheerleaders after a winning game? I was watching TV just last week and saw one Florida cheerleader with tits like two . . . "

Employees usually safe from these higher-learning harangues and interesting sportball asides, cause cautious, scampering little woman and man become blockaded by Bossman Deluxe only once every two-three month. But *supervisors*, ahh, for them it worse: by obsequious necessity they turtles of a slower-moving shell. And Oldcat, being both supervisor and once-ago U of Florida football star, already hear Babylonian math theory four full time since promotion—twenty minute each occasion. Even worser, him pretty sure it not really Babylonians who create base thirteen, but some other ancient foreign creatures. And even worstest?

This all happen before era of corporate raider, so Oldcat and other employees hold no hope of shining buyout knight ever Lear-jetting from Big Apple to sub-divide squished Gainesville orange. Best they can hope for is air-conditionless Volkswagen ride on hot Florida two-lane, dodge armadillos, arrive at apartment, swallow suicidal poison pill of seven hundred or more Bayer aspirin—though of course, Oldcat much too collegiate for that.

"Young man, I'm telling you: all America needs to do is use asterisks for ten, pound signs for eleven, and an ampersand for twelve: it's already on our typewriters: that's the beauty of it. . . . You know, they call it a base thirteen, but that's really misnamed, just like our supposed base ten. Base thirteen changes its decimal point after twelve, just like our base ten changes after nine. You see, it was a lunar-based mathematical system . . . ."

Oldcat, him feel his cheeks going to crack from smiling so much, at so little.

One night, Oldcat working late and so it do happen that Bossman Deluxe there too. Out in shop, Oldcat almost sure the order in front of him have typo in decimal place that change 10,000 to 100,000. This small company in Jellico never buy so many parts before. What, it of sudden manufacturing walkie-talkies for army? If so, too late, for we out of Vietnam more than two year now.

Him need to go ask Bossman Deluxe, but know his Jellico query certainly lead to Babylonian Captivity. (*"Stupid, stupid. This never would happen if we used Babylonian lunar base thirteen instead of our ridiculous base ten. Ten? What are we, Neanderthals who still need to count with fingers and toes?"*)

Oh woe! But go he have to, Oldcat know. . . .

Trudge, trudge, trudge. Oldcat already feel dislocated back tightening in protest as his pupils dilate like they two opposing linemen on steroids.

Bossman Deluxe Brown's office hug darkest corner of building, love-nestled amid thick red carpet, set inside a suite of offices with vines drizzling nitrated water from oversized concrete planters hung on outside wall like—well yes, this so really true—like biblical Babylonians hung their innocent gardens. Ahead of him, Oldcat spies this darkness looming even as he trudge, trudge, trudge down the freshly waxed corridor reflecting flickering, non-biblical fluorescent lights hung overhead. *Wait! Fluorescent not supposed to flicker,* him realize, not daring to look up. *Maybe it just my spinal headache, a migraine aura setting in. Or maybe,* he shiver, *maybe it my soul, like Moses quivering before burning bush. But I no Moses—and Bossman Deluxe certainly no Yahweh God-Father burning in bush: him don't even wear a flammable beard, much less own an all-knowing brain. Hell, he barely even rent a half-knowing one.*

Trudge, trudge, trudge.

Dimness shimmering ahead like from Calcutta's black hole and Oldcat's pupils tearing at eyelids, his arms pumping out goose-bumps in semi-syncopation. Him catch cold, develop eyeball pneumonia if he have to stay too long? Supposed plant-wide joke is that Bossman Deluxe keeps this section of office air freezing so that all secretaries' nipples show.

Trudge, trudge, trudge.

Gesundheit. Oldcat shiver around a corner, thinking of imminent Babylonian lecture: could it be not through sneezes but through nipples and pores that souls go? Him sigh and wish Moses would whoosh from the overhead air-duct to lead him away from Dis-promised Land.

Trudge, trudge, trudge.

With last twist of corridor, lights truly darkened, yet soon Oldcat spot, through latticework concrete blocks, secretary's white sweater dangling on chair. It so limp and sad, like corpse of hung woman at well. Pressing nose against cold concrete block, he feel like bit actor trying out for part in Grade B gangster movie: "Anybody besides us machine-gunned corpses in boondock warehouse?"

" . . . just a little kiss . . ." Oldcat hear in answer smurmuring over blush-red carpet from behind half-open office door inside suite. Then come crack of falling plastic, followed by thud, like phone book full of dead football fans giving up ghosts.

"Mr Brown! I'm engaged, Mr Brown." This woman-voice cut high through dimmed lighting and latticework blocks.

"That doesn't matter. He'll never find out. No one will. Just this once. It'll be like a last fling for you. We really need and appreciate your services here, you know."

Harsh sounds of a swivel chair being kicked out of the way.

"Mr Brown! Please stop! Please!"

High heel bang against door, which snap closed.

Oldcat's eyes glaze as he spot over-large, green something-dendrum next to him, oozing Biblical wrath and sin. He shove both it and concrete planter off wall shelf, like Samson pushing first crumbling pillar. Huge pot break with thunk as hollow as Mr Brown's mathematic theory and soul, for both belong in same empty set.

"Who's out there? What the hell's going on?" This come from behind inner office door.

Oldcat walk to another pot and knock it to floor with same hollow thunk. Philistines, they panicking and screaming now as crushful stone blocks do from temple fall. Cheap plywood door open, and captive secretary run out to grab white sweater and button it tight. Through the lattices of concrete blocks, she spy Oldcat, who not sure what to do but nod.

"I said, what the hell's going on out there, Miss Timberlake? Who the hell's out there?"

She brush her honey-brown hair with fingertips and force a smile toward Oldcat.

"No one. Two of the plants have fallen. I'll go get a janitor to clean them up. Then I have to leave."

"Leave? But we haven't finished the report."

"I can finish it at home."

"Then you might as well stay at home, Miss Timberlake."

"Then you might as well call a janitor yourself."

She grab her purse from desk, snap it shut, strut to emergency exit door in side suite, shove and kick it until alarm sound, smile weakly once more at Oldcat, then slam her leaving.

"Hellfire, you slutty bitch!" That the only sound Bossman Deluxe make; Oldcat hope it a premonition of Bossman's next sexual encounter.

He look at gawping side door and screaming alarm system, then dash down hallway, back to the assembly line.

Funny, but him spine feel better already.

At his own desk, he stare at order for 100,000 transitors. Of previous, him always have impression that Czar Brown make things worse for supervisors, but of sudden him realize that trickle-down effect for hourly employees even worser. And very worstest? That time, it ever arrive, or just dangle in background like some corpse-white sweater strangling in Babylonian Captivity?

That night at home, Oldcat write an out-of-state employer who show interest before. Three weeks later, he hired and can quit Timely. But before him leave he receive a UPS shipment containing one fifth of Old Forester whiskey and one expensive crystal decanter. "Thanks for saving me," the rose-scented note inside read. "I heard through the grapevine about your moving to Alabama and your new job. Good luck."

For the first time in six months of unrequited Daffodil love Oldcat really smile. Leaving building forever that night, him mispurposely knock over another something-dendrum with UPS package. Topsy-turved broken pot resemble Bossman Brown's balding crown, while dirt and sand scamper across floor just like his mad math brain cells—or just like 90,000 extra transistors, which probably be flying back angrily and unpaid from Jellico real soon.

And why not? What trickle down, often prickle right back up.

Norman Vincent's Peal

Oldcat, smelling like deceased coffee pot, travel all night from Florida to new job in Alabama. By dawn he arrive at outskirts of town and thereupon spy two chewing-tobacco farmers tinkering with a Santa-red tractor broken down beside a holly- green "*Welcome to Carpenterville*" sign. He slow, sip last of Selma coffee, and think, *Hah, these X-mas rubes do just fine for me.*

On into town, he approach a greasedy spoon with pig flanks floating from two kitchen ventilators, handsome cigarette smoke oozing from door cracks. Him not dismayed but park car, inspiring self with Norman Vincent Peale positive talk: *You only an egg-y embryo, this only your first stop on way to fame and fortune like Evel Knieval or even O.J. Simpson.* Then he pull up chin and step inside, sit at counter to rest so-tired head in caffeine-stained palms, hear dishes clack dirtily in back, think how fine and healthy two bright-eyed eggs fried over-easy will taste, and doze into . . .

. . . Oldcat watch his body, like a cartoon ghost, pass through iron gates of nearby live-oak cemetery to peer into polished granite stone and prepare its face after longsome journey, to bend to caretaker's faucet and scrub spilt Selma truck stop coffee from its hands, to sit on brown winter grass and put its suitcase in order, to yank irksome hair and make its moustache trim. In quick dream-time it finish, then yawn and lean on tumblestone to cluck at self. "My, how smart I," body announce to air and gravedirt and leftover rainwater. Oldcat, he twitch and want to awake and shout warning, cause body leaning on pink granite not notice deadly red and green velvetsnake sniffing around tumblestone's foot marker. *But velvetsnake notice body all right. And bite. Body slump, without a twitch. That afternoon, a black caretaker accidentally spit chewing tobacco on Oldcat's dead neck, discover corpse's greasy head stuck to electronic parts order form for 100,000 transistors. Caretaker, him know right away. All tumblestones in town read,* **He born on this date, he die of self hate.** *It town's sole poem. Oldcat, you see, stumble on original town of snakes. And snake, he do, oh he do always look out for his own . . . .*

"Whadya want?"

This voice pierce into both eardrums like wicked stepmother's up-and-down sewing machine needles. Startled young Oldcat awake to glance from his unwashed, coffee-ground palms into the bleached eyes and puffed hair of a something-aged waitress.

Her eye whites, what wrong with them? They bulge, they gleam like they stuck in dead preying mantis carcass long clung to barnyard door.

"Well?" Impatient waitress, she bang oily apron into counter and scrape red witchy fingernails—one inch, maybe three long—across

Plexiglas pie cover. As pie cover cry sorrowfully, yellow flakes drop from her nails—hoary skin or stale crumbs? Do it matter which?

Seeing Oldcat looking at falling flakes, an angry wrinkle cocks onto waitress's forehead, like a Colt .45 sniffing for a skull to spatter; then her milky mantis eye whites bulge even more.

"Clos-er! Come clos-er!" their mushroom pupils chant.

Oldcat try to study menu, but what? That curlicue, it a piece of rancid pork rind or her apron string? And look! Some abandoned child, it yesterday endure death heave on her blouse sleeve? She pull something from her hip pocket—Oldcat afraid it may be dirty toilet paper—and unwrap it. Ah, chewing gum. And another surprise: it a fresh stick, not recycled wad. This gum, her witchy red nails stab into, her yellow beaver teeth bite. At same time, her breath dog-paddle down until Oldcat reminded of finer ashtrays he has met.

Gripping the counter's underside, he feels years of gum hidden there, like old love letters and high school yearbooks lingering in moldy closet. It just about all that young he can do to stop himself from windsprinting out front door, all the way back to Florida. He even forget to ask about bathroom and washing up caffeinated hands: what the use, if Witch Hazel going to serve food?

"Whad—" she start again, dropping the gum wrapper to the floor.

"Number four, please," he croak, pointing to the plastic menu caked with enough grits to feed pen full of hungry coon dogs. Oldcat hear noise and look around, thinking maybe there really be bitch in heat baying three, four stools away. But, no, it the town's garbage truck, which doubtless been stopping to deliver here for past six or seventy year.

"Hashbrownsandpan-cakes!" the waitress shout to some perpendicular rhubarb lurking in kitchen. Though Oldcat can see face through gun-slit window he still uncertain whether it belong to male, female, or plant.

"CLACK!" Waitress again bang counter with greasy apron and crack gum in her cavernous mouth. "Number Four. Thadall? Donchu wan' no egg with it?" She poise a yellow stiletto pencil, whose color match her yolky teeth, over order pad.

Yes, what happen to two smiling eggs you originally want, Oldcat of sudden wonder. You have recurring childhood fear of encountering eyeballs of two runny yolks? He ask self as waitress turn to reveal new spot lounging on her tight skirt like some unknown county road. Then he remember seconds-ago snakebite dream and know that he can no longer trust a simple Norman Vincent Peale word like *eggs*. After all, who really ever know into just what they going to hatch? O.J. Simpson just like Evel Knieval: both can leap flying over Hertz counter, but where they going to land? And maybe too, when eggshell break, instead of smiling sunshine egg, hydrogen-sulfide thalidomide abortion will litter stovetop or counter.

Waitress, she call out something to cook, who grunt, its red face looking from this angle less like a rhubarb, more like a wet ptomaine beet. *Egg revelry even spookier than tolling death bell, Norman Vincent,* Oldcat think. *What if those roadside farmers from an hour ago hatch into twin groomsmen at my own wedding, what if this she-creature straddling the greasy floor hatch into my mother-in-law—or—goodawful god!—even my bride.*

Oldcat shake head and swallow. He badly want to wet lips and whistle for Lassie from childhood TV to save him, but that pooch nowhere in sight. Instead, a hovering, milk-white, preying mantis wrist serve him coffee with a click, while mushroom eyes refuse to blink.

My bride? Oldcat think. In that case, I surely scootch on Santa's lap and ask for cool, comforting winter tumblestone and velvetsnake's surprise green and red X-mas bite.

Sleepless Hollow

It dark and moonless outside his Carpenterville bachelor apartment when Oldcat eye yellow-paged paperback called *The Legend of Sleepy Hollow and Other Tales,* which lie flopped on his stark green laminate kitchen table like a dead cat's eye. His new friend Tom been loaning him this and other strange books, since the neither of them can watch TV without encountering major brain hernia.

"Meow," Oldcat call to paperback, and his silly sound echo from threadbare curtains and dirty blinds. But paperback no come to him, though Oldcat wiggle fingers first like mouse's tail, then like catnip coated twine. So he give in and retrieve book, dump self in lumpy, turd-brown imitation La-Z-Boy by window, and torture through reading this old-timey thing, keeping dictionary at eternal hand, to discover in end that spooky Sleepy Hollow story all a joke: bumpkin character Brom Bones, he jealous for local girl and been tricking this newcomer horsebacked schoolteacher named Ichabod with a pumpkin.

Oldcat cogitate: this how maybe I get sure-enough girlfriend? Go riding with infra-red jack-o-lantern in black convertible to the Confederate Widows' tea, upstart some local schoolteacher to become in-law heir to plantation and family fried chicken recipe? Possible, cause there sure plenty plantations around, though mostly they raise catfish, cattle, racism and pine trees, not fried cock-a-doodle-dee's.

But no, that scene not possible on reconsider, cause Oldcat sure there no girls his age living in Carpenterville or whole of Summons County—none even in entire tri-county area—he done searched bars, church socials, cheese hoops in country grocery stores, and shacks in local backwoods, so he know. Probably have to return to Florida palmetto plains to import a belle. There be a tariff fee?

How come anyway, he continue to think on hearing dog bark far off outside, that a smart schoolteacher like Ichabod fall for this dumb pumpkin trick? Maybe his hormones in a fritter because pretty Sleepy Hollow heiress tell him to scoot away, go tumble his horse into some nighttime ditch, see what she care.

Oldcat wish a pretty Summons County girl tell him to do anything: trot out to mah daddy's farm and shovel manure, hurry on downtown with month's paycheck and buy me that pretty pink outfit in Tinker's display window, slouch over at bar in Brass Chimpanzee and drink stale, flat beer from mah dirty high-heel pink prom pump.

Yes ma'am, yes ma'am, Oldcat know he reply, using his most genteel but controlled Kentucky Colonel drool.

No matter though, cause then probably same Ichabod schoolteacher from local junior college come along and steal her back anyway. No pumpkins grow in Summons County—it too damned hot—so what left for with Oldcat to ruse? Cotton bole? Banana peel? Dirty high-heel shoe?

Agh, this all coming out wrong, like worm oozing from poor man's fall-in-ditchside skull. He read this story to get scared and creeped out, and look what happen: him begin to think of hormones.

"You scared all right. You plenty scared."

"Where that come from? Who say that? Who there?" Except for roaches softly clicking their febrile antennae, the apartment loom emptily, and young Oldcat peer out dark window to moonless night. One lone, bone-white dust speck fall from ancient wooden shades, taking so slow to reach floor that him know. Oh yes, him know, all right: it not who there, but who *not* there that really bring on this graveyard fright.

All the News That's Fit To Print

Oldcat awake in bachelor apartment feeling like a Monday newspaper—all typos and bad news. Even the Personal Want Ads read lonely, so many broken hearts searching for SWM's and DWF's. Himself, he search in bathroom mirror only to find UFO, and *that* not likely to attract many comers.

> Handsome UFO, occasional smoker, drinker, pray-er, and police informant looking for attractive SWF, age 21-5. Willing to undergo brain transplant with same.

No, that not gonna flood any postal reply box. Hard, it so hard to be young and have working parts to brain still standing on loading dock in another state. Him like robot Gort in *The Day the Earth Stood Still*: all machinery just clicking, whirring—clacking, waiting, waiting. So, shaking head, he wipe the medicine cabinet mirror clean and frazzle through Monday as he can.

That accomplished, he frazzle through the week, through the month, through the year as he can—work, work; visit folks at old Kentucky home; go out with new friend Tom to bars and look for Ms Right; swear off hangovers; work, work; finally take vacation. All the time, he still feel like typo in some forlorn Personal Want Ad.

It on second year vacation with Tom that he meet Ms Puss, who also vacationing in Florida. He can't believe that she live in Faunsdale on cattle farm, just two towns off from silly Carpenterville: he been long time convinced that all young women banned from tri-county area. Maybe, he even suspected, all young females gobble too much fried chicken and pecan pie and die of young girl heart attack to be buried in local live oak cemetery. Say . . . maybe that, and not equal-time racism, be Alabama's deep Spanish moss secret, he'd thought.

But then, upon meeting Ms Puss amid so many St. Augustine Beach red sands, him immediately stand in front of bathroom mirror again to move his newspapery life from the Personal Want Ads to the Funnies—start out with Apartment 3-G, hope to end with Dagwood and Blondie.

Yes, he marvel as toothpase foam in mouth like spilling champagne. Yes, now he secure and now newspaper life all becoming bold print clear: in high school and college he live on Sports Page. Then after back injury, him live in Want Ads hunting for job; then him slump to Personal Want Ads looking for mate. Now him dance on Funny Page, soon to be on Society Page strutting wedding tux, then with raise be big potbelly entrepreneur on Business Page.

I ever make Front Page News? Agh, no matter: on foggy mornings, let front page be filled with bloody six-car wrecks; on New York Strip evenings, let it flow with politician's lies. I'll keep happy with the supplemental sections B through Z, and an inky obituary which state that I have survivors, that I have survived.

That, mirror, mirror, is all the news that's fit to print.

Spiraling at Warped Speed

After eight years of marriage, Ms Puss begin studying Roman Catholicism since-if they going to send their twins to Carpenterville's Catholic school to avoid the equal-time racisms of the all-white Summons County Christian Academy and all-black Summons County public schools.

"Catholicism, racism—always some *ism* bumming our good world." This Oldcat's only comment as his wife read through Roman Catholic brochures night after October night.

"Umph," Ms Puss reply, spouting a fountain of eloquence.

Funny thing though: Oldcat realize she just then say everything that need to be said, for in autumn, leaves change color; in winter, leaves drop. What you going to do, word-talk them out of their downward spiral? And just so, what you going to do about the world and the thick, sad way it rotate?

So he begin to study Catholicism too, and amid tracts and brochures on one blustery tornado-watch night he ask: "Pope infallible? Cannot never lie? What that supposed to mean?"

"Just what it says, but it happen only when he speak from what's called *ex cathedra* about church matters, not when he discussing how good was tuna fish sandwich for lunch."

"Umph," Oldcat reply.

They two sitting around kitchen table, over bottle of wine while six-year-old fraternal twins thumping somewhere else screaming and fighting to match useless, raging storm outside. Oldcat then take from pile and open one more brochure, this one as old as maybe first or second pope, for it a brittle, gold-foil mosaic picturing some haloed saint, staff in hand, torturing through this world's weary whitewater stream. Oldcat peer closer and smell a must direct from Roman catacombs, or maybe from stream's far shoreline, who know? But what this? Saint a hunchback? No, he bent cause he transporting a chubby child on his shoulders across white-water stream.

Outside, lightning snap in meaningful way that move Oldcat to crinkle eyebrows and shove gold-foil brochure toward Ms Puss, who reply, "Oh that an inoperative statement. He used to be Saint Christopher, a used-to-be patron saint of travelers. Catholics used to carry a medal of him in their cars and on their luggage, but he's no longer real, he was just a myth, so the pope de-sainted him."

Oldcat's mind glint in a tin-foil roil. *De-sainted? That like de-clawed? This something like how Catholics jumble Easter and other feastdays according to moon phases, sunspots, and seasons? Agh, no-no! No-no! Please have pity, Mr Your Highness Pope: not so moveable, but more secure and immoveable.*

"Who's the baby on his back?" Oldcat ask, pointing to gold mosaic.

"That's the Christ Child, he's who St. Chris supposedly carried across that cold and raging stream."

"Ah." Oldcat pull at stubble like he working his way into tight, dark cupboard and afraid he won't never be able to back out. "Ah," he repeat, throat catching. "Child, he been de-sainted too?"

Some whisper, as real as wind bashing the trees outside, urge, *Careful, Oldcat, careful: fungus winter brown always follow dropping autumn leaves. Careful, be careful: last time you walk into cupboard looking like this was in Gainesville, and then a rat-trap clipped half your stubby tail.*

Ms Puss frown at her blasphemous husband and scoot chair back, thinking herself safer near electric socket, grounded or not, than near someone who make joke like that.

De-sainted. Maybe, Oldcat think, *this moveable feast day stuff not all it crackled up to be. Maybe,* he continue to think as he listen to upstairs water running, thunder booming, TV blaring, his son peeing, and his daughter yelling for brother to shut bathroom door, *maybe the Catholic church people not so smart after all, despite pretty Latin. Why moveable and removable? Why not just immoveable, like Mt. Rushmore or Stone Mountain?* Oldcat shiver at thought of ugly Stone Mountain and stupid vacation trip he and Tom take there. Then he look at gold and royal blue mosaic in his hands and imagine poor St. Chris still riding shotgun in some ancient widow's car, forsaken by the Catholic Church as a fairy tale talisman, yet glued permanent on her dashboard by hairspray from her Confederate Daughter's meeting. But then, would they even let Roman Catholics in? . . . Moveable and removable—what kind of religious solution that to offer for confused human brain?

"Hey, wait just a minute," he blurt, shoving wine glass toward pile of brochures on table. In one paw he shake the brochure, in other he tick off points: "One: If some long-ago Pope declared St. Chris a saint, then two: How can some now-time Pope can say he not? Logic, Ms Puss, logic. One Pope must be lying, no? And both supposed to be in-foul-able, yes? Both supposed to be speaking ex-cathedral, yes?"

"*Ex cathedra.*"

Ms Puss say this and glare. She reach for wine bottle to pour in Oldcat's glass, since they been told they need to drink wine to be good Catholics and since she figure wine gargling in husband's mouth keep him from talking Doubting Thomas questions.

Upstairs, their son flushes the toilet and turns off the water, slams the door to scream back at his sister. Lightning flashes, leaves drop, a branch cracks. Outside on porch, halloween lantern, it just grin on. How ever it able to keep lit in all this wind?

Oldcat clutch brochure and think: *Please, Your Highness Pope, please: no more moveable and removable. That too much for human brain cells. We poor humans need patron saint of travellers back. We all too much like autumn leaves swept by out-of-season tornado, spiraling from Kansas to who-know-where, at warped speed. Please your Highness Pope, please . . . wine fine, but just this once use your cathedral voice and speak, even if it only come out a tailless mouse's squeak.*

Televangelists, Reichstag Fires, and Krazyglue, OR The San Andreas Fault Squared

Oldcat sit at bar in Oysterhead Lounge waiting for Monday Nite Football and listening to pretty blonde teacher sob to boyfriend: "Today," she say, "a little 17 year old girl named Rita came and told me about finding her aunt dead in bed this weekend, her head shotgunned inside-out by her drunken boyfriend, blood spattered on the wall and nightstand. But all this little seventeen-year-old girl worried about was her toddler niece crying in the next room and how this was going to affect *her* for the rest of *her* life." Bombshell blonde teacher stop to take drink—whole bar listening wide-eyed now. "This seventeen-year-old girl put a bloody sheet over her aunt's blasted head and ran to the toddler who was whimpering on the other room's bed. Seventeen-year-old Rita thought she'd better get out of the house since she didn't know where the boyfriend was, so she wrapped the girl in a blanket and hurried to the neighbor's." The bombshell teacher take another drink here and pause to study dead deer antlers hung behind bar. "Rita, she sat in my office telling me this so calmly, just like she was explaining why she didn't have her homework or couldn't make debate team practice. Still worrying only about her toddler niece. Me, I wasn't calm, I was terrified: *Good God, these are all crazed, pacing animals that I'm teaching, each of them from a broken home and rotting streets. The entire pack could turn on me any minute, just like hyenas,* I thought."

Teacher sobbing now, and Oldcat plus entire bar lean forward just like stuffed deer head, to sniff out blood, hatred, love—what?

"I put my arm around the girl," blonde teacher continue, "I put my arm around her, but all the time I was thinking, *Get out of this office, Judy. Get out before that boyfriend drives to this school with an Uzi in his pocket. Quit and take courses in accounting or computer programming—anything, but get out.*" Oldcat here straighten as teacher bang her wine glass on bar. "I'm so ashamed," she say. "That brave teenager worrying about her niece while all I worried about was myself. I don't deserve to be a teacher, to have a license. I don't deserve it."

Boyfriend pat teacher's back; bartender, she pat her hand. Other customers say, "No, no, you just . . ."

Oldcat stare at beer. Him see this bombshell blonde in here before and always think: *Bimbo.* Now him sorry as dried black ink that he ever thought that. Maybe he no deserve to be human, to carry driver's license claiming he same.

Then him stop and look at deer antlers staggering over the bar. This what we now about in America? All barsit and dump on selves, forget little nieces and evil boyfriends? **Him** no gonna worry like this. **Him** gonna brag downtown how he shot that aunt bitch right in her damned cranium. And what about our children in our schools? Teacher right: they all from broken home in which only thing fixed is TV.

Oldcat for once forget sportball game and down beer to trudge home a confused man. In *Walpurgisnacht* bed him feel a low, crooked rumble and begin to sweat. Him blink into darkness. Nextbodydoor, Ms Puss snore. On this terrible night her snore not lilt peacefully, but lurch like a crazed wild boar crashing through an evil forest in search of blood pudding, brain stew, and kidney pie. And all around the ranch house neighborhood they live in, John Woods nature prints shimmy on living room walls, electric garage doors open/close, toilets gargle, cats yowl, children scream, windows crack.

It just like the San Andreas Faultline extending itself across America to slip Texas, Oklahoma, Ohio, Alabama, Tennessee, Virginia, and every inbetween GoodTown, U.S.A., into the dank brine sea. Soon, soon in earthquaked frenzy of hatred, all Americans will lose license to be human. Soon *Walpurgis* melt to *Kristallnacht,* and it be too late for anything but some ranting televangelist Hitler, *Reichstag* fires in Washington, D.C., and Krazyglue welding hatred into Everyville and every me-first brownshirt me.

Feminist Deconstruction

It rain so hard one night that Ms Puss think she Ms Noel. Her imagine standing on Ark's gangplank, say, "Hurry, hurry, you animal." She think, looking over long gruesome line and all them claw fights and ripe rump droppings: *Maybe what if I forget to take a few, and in that way repair Godman's plan—which obliviously not work all great shakes anyhoodle or there be no need of Flood, yes?*

So she kick elephant turd overboard with a grunt and plan plans to work Godman's action a little better. After all, maybe if she just stick to losing a trio of pesky animals, Godman not notice: A: She gonna squash them two mosquito when they flitter all dandylike up plank. Just cause male sip nectar, so what? Plenty birds and bees do that. Bees? Hmmmm. No, leave bee be. The real B. be snakes. Yes, snake done got us into lot of trouble once time, and him ever since slink about all lowlike looking for ankles, rabbits, or mousies. Mousies and rabbits pretty furry nice—and ankles just fine, thank you. Yes, that snake gonna drop. How it reproduce, anyhoodle? Where its thingy? Maybe its thingy really be its whole body. Mr Noel sometime think his thingy be his whole body after all.

Ms Noel laugh at that, but her laugh not funny. Rather, her eyes slit lowlike as two deer strut by and plank clatter. She peer through large rack of moving antlers toward Mr Noel on fo'c's'le screaming and swearing at Ham, Japheth, and Shem. Him then trip over crocodile tail and rip up ark plank to throw at Daughter Number One who only bending down to reassure confused mama crocodile, who herself after all only trying to locate proper hatch to go in.

Why is it, come to think, that Mr Noel no give names to their daughters, anyway? Calling them One, Two, and Hey You!, not particularly nice. And why him even want stupid crocodile on board if he so clumsy him going to trip over such an obvious green tail?

Ms Noel count more animals and sweep overboard more dung: then she notice her three sons throwing coiled rope at Daughters Number Two and Hey You! just as Mr Noel had at Number One. One daughter scream and fall, and sons laugh.

Ms Noel's breasts rise against the coming rain, her eyelashes squeeze until they slice wet air like knife blades. Her look backwards at mucus green clouds tumbling toward ark, her look forward at fo'c's'le and Mr Noel gripping wine bottle in one hand while shoving ark's detached wheel with his shoulder, trying to jam it back on the tiller—him must have had crocodile tantrum and ripped wheel off when she wasn't looking. She press hands to throbbing temples as Mr Noel angrily heave wheel overboard: Now he done it. How we ever going to steer to Mt Ararat?

Somewhere. Somewhere on other side of Mr Noel's wine-drunk ranting and those menacing rainclouds float moonbeams, she think. Her hear from sailor stories how worst sea storms always visit at night, maybe have something to do with moonbeams seeding clouds, no one knows—but no matter either, for it sworn to be true.

Ms Noel suddenly remove hands from throbbing temples. Yes, she think. No matter that the tiller torn. She know how to steer.

For, enlightened, she's envisioned the most lovely, most seaworthy C to fill out her deadly trio, the final link to turn Godman's plan perfect, just as it should be: Yes, one typhoony Monday Football night when Shem, Japheth, Ham, and Mr Noel out on quarterdeck in their winecups and shivering their tall timbers, she and Daughters One, Two, and Hey You! will padlock all the hatches. Sooner-later, all four males will wash overboard to join mosquito and snake, adding final C to A + B.

No more males. Ms Noel sway like happy mast in wind and pat purring Bengal tiger on snout while humming to self and envisioning that happy, peaceful test-tube baby sea.

—Of sudden, Ms Puss awake, hearing Oldcat pull into driveway after Oysterhead Lounge night. It still raining to beat Flood outside, and she sure garage door going to stick, cause Oldcat been promise to phone the repairman for at least eleventy-five weeks. SCREE-chunk! It do stick and she hear Oldcat stumble-curse from car, to lift the door himself. GRU-unk! GRU-unk! She giggle, wondering what happen if he not get it open. Maybe she collect double indemnity after him wash into street's sewer drain. Her then remember dream and Ms Noel standing on deck petting the Bengal tiger: And just who say women can't be practical? Ms Puss chortle. Test-tube baby sea? Yes, that good Biblewoman's plan certainly promise more efficient future than any Godman's shimmering, lying rainbow.

Big Boat

Oldcat, him dreamble one night: *Big boat a-comin. Big boat a-comin.* In this dream, darkness glimmer more than do light until he see only moony knife-prow of boat loom high above what must be his own insignificant sunless head. Look! Isn't that him standing out on a black, slippery dock? Maybe so, for all around, waves lap their nasty shadow-wet sound and spew their nasty cold white foam to make the night roam like an angry murderer's cloak.

Ahoooooo, ahoooooo, whisper the big boat, still a-comin, like it no care about no damn thing in world. But why all else so quiet? Why?

In dream him no see barnacles—him no see much anything—but yet him afraid to lean left nor right, for him do imagine sharp wetsalt barnacle mouths gaping somewhere below to gash him toes, ankles, and heels. In fact, him so afraid that he won't even lift a quiet paw for fear cold air slice it. Him remain so still that he imagine himself enchained like Prometheus bound, except he nowhere near so smart—only fire he ever start was in athletic dorm with Bic lighter and pepperoni pizza fart.

Ahoooooo, ahoooooo, whisper Big Boat, nearer, nearer, chopping through water in most mean and unstoppable way. Big Boat no laugh at jokes or pranks, it no laugh at football victories or dizzy English professors. It no laugh at fat marijuana cigarettes or stupid sit-coms. It no laugh at no damned thing. And them bloody dark waves, parting before it: they lap, they lap, they lap . . . .

"What it mean?" shout Oldcat next rosy-dawn, fumble-finger morn when him awake. He in bed alone, Ms Puss, she already up. Oldcat's stomach sick, so he walk downstairs and drink coffee. Stomach now sicker. He tell dream to Ms Puss, who suddenly politest toast butterer in universe—*scritch, scritch*. Polite or not, each scritch eat Oldcat's calcifying vertebrae one by one. What dream mean? he whimper to self.

"What it mean?" he ask Ms Puss.

"Eat your toast and jam, Oldcat. Hush, you wake children with all this dream talk about a boat coming to fetch you."

*Ahoooooo, ahoooooo.*Oldcat nearly fall off stool looking out window.

Ms Puss bring over toast and when he bite it, the crunch nearly shatter ten-twenty teeth, so him dunk next bit in coffee. "Need quiet," he mutter, "need much quiet."

Ms Puss, she stare out window and scritch, scritch.

Sunday come, it go. . . .

Monday morning, he tell a supervisor, he tell secretary, he tell friend Tom about big boat dream; at night, he even go to Oysterhead Lounge and tell Monday Nite Football Loungers. What it mean, he ask and ask. Everybody polite-like smile, then change subject fast as squirrels changing tree limbs. Maybe they too all had this big boat dream? Oldcat wonder.

"Was they any fish you could catch in your dream sea?" ask friend Tom.

"No, it was too dark, too cold." Oldcat twirl ice-coldest mug bartender Pat have, leave paw print all over, wish he ordered hot chocolate instead.

"What it mean?" he whimper half to self, half to . . .

But Tom no answer, just stare at bartender Pat's cigarette tip glowing and her red hair prettying. In background junior college student slap nearly antique pinball machine and make it tilt.

All this time, garlic-heavy pepperoni blood sump its sea voyage through Oldcat's heart. . . . *Ahoooooo, ahoooooo,* until Oldcat shiver like black-dog delirium tremens.

He know what dream mean. Oh yes, he know.

"We all do," he say to no one in particular, though maybe his gaze rest mostly on bony antler rack hovering too pal-sy and familiar-like over the bar. Antler-bone, it certainly know. But though calcium always kiss, it never yet tell.

Immoveable, Moveable, Removable

One morning at job Oldcat pretend-work at his so-important vice-presidential desk to investigate an eternal calendar and learn just what day of the week was January 27, 19-and-umpedy, his illustrious birthday. . . .

A Monday.

He so happy that he have to blow nose. Monday! Now he, especial of all people, can begin every week with his exclusive immoveable feast birthday just like the Catholics he been studying. Him already been fantasizing his own liturgical calendar of immoveable feasts: each Sunday hold Easter's resurrection and peace, each Thursday a taste of turkey and thanksgiving. And say instead of Labor Day coming only on the first Tuesday of September, him further cogitate, wiggling toes and smelling coffee as he hear people outside in large office really working, what if it become the immoveable Tuesday of each and every week? That way all Americans wiggle toes and fry picnic mullet four days a month, ha-ha.

But the more him seriously ponder this immoveable celebration idea, the more him want to privately designate each day with its own aura like the saintly days of feast. And with his latest birthday discovery, how wonderful the lineup would be: Monday his birthday, Tuesday a fish day, Thursday filled with 24 hours x 60 minutes of thanks, Sunday be life and peace, and of course, Friday somehow must work out to be a complete day of frivolity.

His little mind spin and spin to complete personal liturgical schedule through lunch hour. Over half-warm cafeteria salmon croquettes him complete all liturgical week and weekend too.

. . . So when Monday arrive Oldcat hold his first calendar practice in bathroom before mirror: *Today, some-so year ago, was handsome I born. Wunnerful Wunnerful! Girls, please will you pour the delicate pink bubbly and sing a lively song, while the funked accordion player a polka do play along? Happy birthday to me, Happy birth—*

"Dad? What are you doing?"

Oldcat startle-look at his little boy Grrr standing out in the hall, blonde hair dazzling like noonday sun. My hair once like that, Oldcat think. Then he look back to mirror and see his hand propped on own head, gripping a gray hair like it a ripcord to a time machine. He give gray hair a yank and the bathroom mirror immediately chant, "You so much handsomer that way, brother. Younger too."—But wait, how can that be if today, Monday, celebrates him own immoveable feast birthday? He not younger, he one week nearer gravesite. *The worms crawl in, the worms crawl out, the worms play pinochle on your—*

"Dad?"

Humph.

Maybe this immoveable stuff not all it cracked up to be, if it deliver 52 birthdays a year. Maybe him just should stick to facing Grim Reaper once on January two-seven.

"Dad!"

Oldcat remember how him father, the big Civil War buff, jokingly want to give teenaged Oldcat son the middle name of "War Order Number One" cause January 27 the day that Lincoln issue that same proclamation during Civil War. "*W.O.R.N.*O! That's what we could nickname you, boy! But then someone would shorten it to *Porno*, wouldn't they?" Oh yeah, that funny and fine, have big joke, Pop. And your nickname backward or forward still make you a soda, jerk.

"Dad!?"

But Oldcat prefer any nickname to "Monday Blues," which is what he be calling self if he celebrate a birthday every immoveable Monday.

"PO-O-P!" Grrr insist, pulling angrily at Oldcat's Fruit-of-the-Loom underwear and letting its elastic pop in his own version of anti-paternal pun.

Oldcat yelp. Grrr lunge for underwear again, but Oldcat too fast and swivel away. How many more times he be quick enough to escape rising son? Not many, if every Monday bring an immoveable birthday celebration.

"Da-ad, come on. I have to . . . I want in."

"Shhh. Me hypnotizing self to forget what day Monday is."

Grrr make fist and hit at air to say, "That's stupid. That's really stupid. Grownups never make any sense. I don't never want to grow up."

"Ever," Oldcat absently correct Southernism, though he wonder: *Is that the whole point? Maybe instead of making birthdays an immoveable feast, we should make them re-moveable.* Yes, remove every birthday and feastday until we never hear even Big Ben's ticks or tocks. . . .

"Da-a-ad! I have . . . to . . . go!"

Go? Oldcat float single gray hair to waste can and walk out, trying to snap his son Grrr's underwear, missing as the boy rushes in and slams the door. Well, at least sister will be happy, cause she won't hear fraternal twin tinkle.

Go. Oldcat stand still and listen to toilet lid lift; then hear Grrr twist on the faucet so no one will hear him peeing, a year-old habit Ms Puss and Oldcat trying to break after sister make so much fun one day at school. Freud never had mean twin sister or he would understand more about potty-training. *It okay, Son. Like winter leaves, we all have to go,* Oldcat think, trying not to shuffle his bare feet on the static-red cold carpet.

So maybe, he continue to think as he listen to water running and his son peeing, so maybe the Catholic church people pretty smart after all: moveable, immoveable, and removable—last like poor St. Chris abandoned in an icy mid-stream, like poor lanksome President Lincoln, who never lived to issue Peace Order Number One. Just as well, Oldcat think, cause someone would have shortened it to *Porno.* Moveable, immoveable, and removable. Wading saints, swimming fish, jumping assassins, dying presidents, lousy plays, and immature jokester fathers—all tumbling in the raging stream of life.

Gllggg, gllggg. Toilet flush in agreement.

Moveable, immoveable, and removable. Who ever thought a toilet bowl could be so smart?

Tuesdays

Sound and Fury

Oldcat, in high school and college, play sportball until his brains drop. Oh yes, even when him make minuscule fart or burp, all stadium clap. Soon, girls swoon tears, boys pet his rear, women leer, men buy him beer. Oldcat, him ARRIVE, to become Sportballer Deluxe.

He one time in high school hear rumor that brussels sprouts be brain food, so he jock-hop in pick-up to hoe down whole unseasonable patch. He imagine self to swagger into town and toss dead brussel sprouts this-way-that, till people sigh, *My, my, look at that strutting young handsome Oldcat; we should cheer, we should name big building and green grass field to honor such handsome creature.* And in college, young he further imagine that him soon own university, steakhouse, and two used car lot just like many other famous Gainesville sportballers he can name. Himownself will be biggest of all, himownself will land biggest of all contract on TV, which will showcase closeup of himownself's biceps, triceps, accompanied by sound bits of himownself's magnificent burps and farts. Common people of the nation will become so happy they faint, so happy they push nose to Rose-Bowl, Super-Bowl screen in hope to sniff young Oldcat's sweat. College president, banker, lawyer, mayor, Indian chief—all man-nation will dream-wish they could be young Oldcat. Himownself soon to become so saintly that if he deign endorse a rubber tree tennis shoe, young admiring folk in street will carry razor or gun and kill for same smelly commodity. Yes yes, all America will see that it good and do . . . .

Alas, soon after this dream young Oldcat hurt knee once when him stupidly stumble over cubic centimeter of wet artificial turf, then hurt back twice when him flounder under what seem like seven thousand raging, moldy jock straps of opposing Florida State U team. Him lick last hurt, have doctor, nurse and lion trainer lick—still hurt, still bad. Girlfriend and stray young brunette cheerleader both wave pom-poms over broked back: it still big bad news.

Three months later, mid-year senior Oldcat wrinkle like tanned pigskin. Him fart once, then broken line stumble into nearby Payne's Prairie—wherein which quiet swamp no sportball announcer perch even on cypress stumps to provide color or play-by-play. So, while sprawling fanless and girlfriendless atop dirty mosquito weeds and beside sharp palmetto fronds Oldcat can almost hear loud cheer from Gainesville football stadium—but the shissh of nearby slinking water moccasin and burrowing armadillo screech even louder, so him whimper and pull goldenrod into a quilt over face, hope that flower not hay fever him to death like he been transformed into some allergic pencilneck professor. Ghostly cheersound bounce off sky in its rise from far-off Gainesville stadium again—but cheersound not for him, he know: it for some young, healthy sportballer.

Only sound for Oldcat?

Achoo!

Road Map

Oldcat, when teenager, work with funny girl. They share silly crush, but really, this girl be his first-time other-sex friend. She as Italian as olive oil and pasta, and tell Mafia/Pope jokes in office all the time. "Oldcat! Did you hear about the nun who went fishing with the Pope? . . . Oldcat! Did you hear about the Mafia Boss who bought his daughter a Volkswagen? . . ." Her two rouge cheeks jounce so merrily that they make Oldcat and everyone happy, even when her jokes do not.

Oldcat and funny girl all the time go out, fake i.d. and pitcher beer together in a big group; they hug; Oldcat happy to rub her Italian *mama-mia's*; funny girl happy to pat Oldcat's young sportballer rear-to-endum.

Both smart enough to grab those items anyway. Oldcat, he introduce funny girl to all male friends, including jock-o all-state quarterback;

she introduce him to all female friends, including va-va-voom Italian exchange student. But neither smart enough to grab one of those . . . or even one another.

The whyfore that they no fall in love, raise gangsters and attend operas? Him too stupid to learn Italian, it seem; and her keep mind of own.

You think you know how this story end? Then you just like teenaged Oldcat, who think he strap Official Rand McNally Road Map of Life in jock-tight back pocket and of consequent know everything and how it end.

Here what happen: Italian girl meet charming Italian boy—obliviously not one of Oldcat's Ameruhcan football friends. Oh happy happy this operatic couple seem to be. Boong bang bong! O duo mio! In six week, maybe less, they engaged. Oldcat, he jittered and speak to funny girl alone: "You sure you know man well enough?" he ask, fumbling for words, finding right ones for once in life. Funny girl, she get huffed. "What do you mean by that? Of course I do," she answer. "Oldcat, you act like a tough jock, but you're really just a mother hen."

Wedding come, Oldcat attend. Listen, it so Italian-y beautiful in big cathedral church with funny girl's thin, lovely, raven-haired soprano exchange student friend singing "Ave Maria" that young Oldcat have three tears accordion from garlicked eye.

That night though, terrible strange things happen. You try to guess, Oldcat could not:

Okay, Italian duo-mio in car wreck and die in each other arms?

No.

Okay, they go to wrong hotel and acid-head teenager steal trousseau?

No.

Okay, Mafioso have long-standing blood oath, stick dead horse in wedding bed?

No again.

Okay. Trojan-enz Rubber break and they bake pizza pie twins on first night?

No, no and no. Give up? May as well. Road map too strange.

Right after wedding Oldcat prance downtown to bar, show fake i.d., and talk with flighty queerbo friend who so far out of closet that chartreuse moth-dust glow on his shoulders, ruby pomegranate blossom on his luscious full lips. Oldcat tell this friend about wonderful Italian wedding, high-note *Ave* song (which Oldcat imitate to much giggles), drafty Catholic incense, royal-regal priest in pretty white silk robe, and all the fancy *omini-domini's* floating in perfumed air.

"E-eeeeeew. Who got married?" queerbo friend ask.

Oldcat tell.

"What? You're kidding! He's the biggest fag in town!"

Oldcat blink, like cocksure jock who run touchdown in wrong direction, score safety for opposing team. Oldcat say name again, say what groom do, say how he look, knowing there some honest mistake.

"I'm telling you: he's the biggest fag in town!"

Oldcat look to friend's lover, who not too sure of leaving chartreuse closet, but have to speak B + W truth now. He nod, then shake head like sad construction crane swinging wrecking ball toward antebellum library.

Oldcat want to cry, want to shout. Him sick. His goodest and onliest girl who be his sametime friend just marry a lying jerk who somereason make her for fool. Punching bag, punching bag, young Oldcat think.

Too late to tell now, since girl and jerk on honeymoon. Why groom no join army, wash peter with boys all time, leave good Italian girl alone?

Hey, this crazy story have happy end?

Listen. If so, you say, for Oldcat afraid to judge: Girl, she find out, Catholic-Italian marriage annulled. Maybe Mafia do shoot jerk, Oldcat no know, can only hope and donate pocket change to Sicilian branch of NRA.

But happy end? Oldcat, now in his prime of so wise-dom, try to be smart enough to realize that happy ends play only on sitcom TV, that reading road maps to life as useless as pocketing snotty napkin left on all-nite diner table when waitress not looking.

So throw Rand-McNally away. After all, there no 24-hour terrestial maintenance crew on duty, and any titillating earthen road taken eventually going to tangle-tingle, tittle-tattle, topple-tipple, tumble-turn, truncate-turbulate, twist-torture, tyrannize-trounce . . . until only T-verb left is trephine.

Look it up. You see how tender and true the unpredictable turnpike always do that verb every other Tuesday too. . . .

A House Divided

"I can't stand it!" Ms Puss one Tuesday shout.

"What? What?" Oldcat ask, running from bedroom to top of stairs. He home early from work to let plumber in, Ms Puss just come in front door from grocery shopping and own part-time job.

"Two school buses, Oldcat," Ms Puss call up, hugging brown grocery sack and purse. "That's what. Two, when there should only be one."

Oh boy. Oldcat, he know what about to come.

"Little black kids on the public school bus, half of them glaring at me like I'm a white she-devil; little snooty white kids on the academy bus, half of them no-doubt glaring at every black woman they pass like she's escaped from Zululand with a poison blow gun. I can't stand it! I can't stand it!"

Just then plumber clunk something deep in the underbowels of their house, and Oldcat tipple finger toward light switch, waiting for the inevitable static shock to unload from this Daylight-Losing-Time winter evening. He know that it come no matter how careful he be not to shuffle his Wal-Mart sold, but maybe someday something good also come, maybe static startle a neuron here, an axon there, and deliver him insightful solution to the whole world, or at least to Summons County and its racial problems. . . .

But, surprise: no shock.

He hold out calming hand toward Ms Puss, who still flustering atomically at bottom of stair. "All right, you win, you're right. We'll make a tomorrow appointment and visit dandruffed priest to see about sending them to the Catholic school."

Catholic. Brr, as if day not chilly and dark enough.

Oldcat, he raised semi-Methodist, so singing spirituals and eating pot-luck most he know about God and church. He been to a Catholic wedding when him soul sung young and that experience warp weird, like maybe demons and ghosts fling any moment out from incense and climb talons-out up cathedral arches. Besides that, him see *The Exorcist* seven-come-eleven time and know: *Satanas fuge.* Catholic, brr.

But the Catholic school in Carpenterville does at least promote some mix of race, and though this stairwell discussion happen long time before political correctum, who need bird-spined academics to instill a conscience? Most people get one issued early enough, maybe even at birth. So Oldcat touch light switch once more—no shock once more—and resignedly walk down steps to help carry in groceries, while plumber continue to adjust bowels of house.

Waaaang! Waaaang!

"Only Catholic I ever knew was . . . well . . ."

"The Italian girl, right? And all the incense, right?" Ms Puss ask as she set bags on cabinet in kitchen. And when Oldcat nod, she say, "She probably more Italian than Catholic, or maybe she Italian-Catholic and that different from American Catholic."

Oldcat grimace, staring at four steaks he just unbag in kitchen. "You're an optimist," he tell Ms Puss in addendum while holding up steaks, "If you think weather going to turn warm enough to cook out."

"Oldcat, listen to me. If you never knew one other than her—and you liked her plenty well enough, you've told me—just how weird do you think they can be? Catholics, I mean." Ms Puss walk to take steaks from Oldcat's hand. "And this is just November, you know. There'll be plenty more warm weather. Remember, we live in the Deep South, not Kentucky."

"You telling me." Immediately him sorry to say that, cause Ms Puss latch back onto dual school problem.

But maybe it not just deep South, Oldcat think as she talk and plumber in basement waaaang, waaaang. This brotherly love a hard road for all America to travel: just read newspaper, watch TV to see if not so. Our only hope is some Paul Bunyan plumber come rearrange all our deepest pipes, make us drain and think right. Criss-cross here, elbow here, plumber's putty here, and soon axons and neurons flow just right. . . . But then, plumber usually arrive too late, after toilet overflowed, drain clogged, floorboards warped, and house done expired into dry rot.

"Will I have to learn Latin?" Oldcat ask, placing potatoes in bin, seeing whitened eyes from two old ones staring blankly back at him.

"Oldcat, the kids don't even have to become Catholics. We've been through that."

Waaaang! Waaaang!

Ms Puss jump as plumber bang another pipe. "How long's he going to be down there, anyway? Surely he'll be done by the weekend."

"'It's a serious problem you got here, mister.' That's all he told me." Oldcat pull frozen French-style green beans from sack, know that Grrr not going to like them. "How long's it going to be before we have only one school system and racial harmony? As my dad used to quote from Lincoln: 'A House divided against itself cannot stand.'"

"For someone with such dad problems, you sure do quote him a lot." Ms Puss comment from refrigerator.

"I'm quoting Lincoln, not Dad."

Waaaang! Waaaang!

Ms Puss turn on radio, loud. End of weather forecast predict warming by Friday, and she shout "Ha!" either at Oldcat or Lincoln or plumber or Carpenterville racists—who can be sure?

"And Lincoln could have added that fixing a house's plumbing takes a long time, so there's no use in us dividing over that fact."

"Oldcat," Ms Puss say in sweet sing-song that nearly match plumber's waaaang as she lift self-starting charcoal briquets from sack. "Oldcat, honey, you should quit your engineering job at Timely Electronics and enroll in the junior college to become a poet or philosopher, you so smart. Honest." She then shake briquets at him: "Just as long as you let me be the weather forecaster."

Tammy Wynette come on radio and Ms Puss groan: she hate that singer ever since "Stumble by Your Man" come out.

"Plumber, he do America a lot more good than either three," Oldcat comment.

"Either three?"

"Philosopher, poet or weatherman. Of them, plumber, he do most good."

"Weather*man*? He-plumber? What about weatherwoman, or she-plumber or philosopheress?"

Waaaang! Waaaang! Plumber hammer on pipe connected to kitchen sink with sound glarious enough to jump mold around faucet, make Ms Puss drop sack of briquets onto tile floor.

Gentleman Oldcat quickly bend and they both clonk heads and laugh.

"Er-ess? She-he?" Oldcat rub his head, notice several a-sexual stars spinning. ". . . Yes, I agree. That a large part of American plumbing problem too." He sit down on tile, realizing how much his head hurt. Ms Puss do the same and their feet touch.

"Both our heads obviously hard as one another."

"You mean, as hollow," Ms Puss say, joking.

Oldcat grin. "As hard. That much a given guaranteed to be equally shared, regardless of race, sex or creed."

Bogeyman

Oldcat, before Japanese takeover when him become bigshot at Carpenterville plant, have Southern boss who always pick patriotic nose in elevated office window like he table model on display for Mr Universe, Special Lowlife Category.

This boss's bald head shine even under fluorescent tubes of office as he everlastingly eyeball outward to catch some slacker Summons County employee snoozing on assembly line or some ingrate pilfering electronics part, maybe even sneaking whole colored TV into hip pocket—people can do, you know, boss him always remonstrate to Oldcat as if talking to dog or guinea pig in tête à pet. Yes, some people can do just about anything they put a dirty mind to, boss him continue, plucking air and thinking himself ancient Greek philosopher who just happen to stand in momentary exile outside the vineyard. Oldcat always squinch toes and wince, for him stomach afraid boss's finger going to travel to pluck ripe green, but not-so philosophical, grape from nose, even before him very eyes.

You think this a disgusting image of life? Ha. Just wait, Pedro, you ain't seen nada yet. Just how long you been alive, anyway? One, two hour?

One day boss suffer heart attack square-slam in middle of public nose-excavating session. Oldcat, him no observe, but friend Tom say he indeed watch nose, finger and boss's bald head all three flip backwards in swivel chair to disappear from evitable cliff.

Two employees carry boss down stairs and plop on concrete floor like they placing shot deer on display at taxidermy shop. People gather-stare, and Oldcat absently, sadly wonder about the saying "dead as a doornail." Him know what dead mean: it wallow stark before him. But what's a doornail? It somehow opposed to other type nail, say windownail?

Then Oldcat notice one, two, threemore shoulders shake. They laugh? How can this be, all that going on considering? Then he too see and understand: from ex-boss's right nostril hang half-plucked, green philosophical grape.

Oldcat spot oily rag sticking from nearby worker's pocket, grab it and pluck grape, then drop both in trashcan that read, "Hazardous Material ONLY."

As he look back at bossman's already whitening and bloodless rubbery nose, he lean on trashcan and close eyes, himself quick reconsidering whole situation: dead as a doornail.

Oh, him suppose he can guess what doornail is all right—something metallic, rusted, and chunky to support any wooden framework normally providing means of egress and ingress. But that first part, "dead,"—it slam brain like a terrible sand-blind sphinx, for even the finest of all

Greek philosophers never decipher *that* Bogeyman until it entirely too late.

The Joke

Ms Puss twenty-four year old when fraternal twins Meow and Grrr born. When Meow nine, Ms Puss tell daughter old saw about how little girl catching up, soon going to pass her mamma:

"When you one year old, I was twenty-four times as old. Now I'm just a bit more than three times as old. Next, I only be twice as old, and soon you'll pass me and Dad both."

Meow take this so serious, with such a frightened look that Ms Puss have to say it only a ha-ha joke, that Dad and Mom always be older than her and Grrr, and that they always take care of them, not to worry.

Next year, Meow remember this conversation and have big laugh at her and Grrr's birthday celebration. "Soon, Grrr, we're going to be as old as Mom and Dad, and we'll have to go to work to take care of them." Grrr fake shoot his sister with his .22 caliber index finger as she try to explain the complicated math of it. Then she blow out his candles, he blow out hers, and they together lick chocolate and vanilla frosting until they resemble monkeys testing greasepaint for a theatrical company.

Two years later, Meow break arm in back yard one day before birthday. Ms Puss come home from grocery store, hear white-faced Grrr try to explain accident, go into irrational, angry panic when she learn that Oldcat simply drive their little girl to hospital and leave Grrr at home to tell mom what happen.

"Which hospital?" she scream at son, though Carpenterville only have one.

She and Grrr drive to hospital with melting grocery in car, find out that Meow okay. "What you doing with her anyway?" Ms Puss shout at Oldcat in shiny, sterile hospital hallway outside the room. Black janitor look up, hum spiritual and slap mop, no doubt glad to see someone fight besides himself and wife.

"We just were climbing a tree," Oldcat answer, as Grrr lean close to mother.

"Just!"

Luckily for Oldcat, important-looking doctor walk by on shiny floor and nearly slip.

Six week later, when Meow supposed to get cast off, same important-looking doctor find she have infection and place her in hospital again, with IV pumping antibiotic into her heart.

Her heart? Oldcat and Ms Puss share wide-eyed panic like they been invaded by battalion of trolls from tree.

"She going to be all right, Doctor? She just have first period one week before all this happen," Ms Puss tell doctor while they standing on that same shiny floor, though it dry this time. "Is this going to affect her reproductive?"

"If she makes it through this, she'll be fine." Doctor carelessly clack clipboard and carefully walk into Meow's private room.

IF? He already tell them that little girl sick with infection, could lose arm, but he not before this tell them *IF.* Troll, it shouting its hollow-mouthed, goblin worst now and waving large, rusty scythe. Ms Puss frown at male doctor's back going into room, then walk and stare out hospital window at traffic driving by.

IF.

Horns honk, turn signals signal. She think: How stupid like ants we are, crawling on tree limbs, no stop for fallen sister, just come back in morning or on return trip to eat her carcass later.

Doctor come out of room, look at floor to check if it wet, give fake grin, then Ms Puss go in.

"Mom?"

Ms Puss smile to see daughter smiling from ugly hospital bed, holding up a gray pocket calculator from school like she holding a atomic scientist's slate.

"Mom, I'm twelve and one-sixth years old now. And you're only thirty-six. You're not even three times as old as me anymore. I figured it out: I really am catching up." And Meow giggle.

Ms Puss walk to bed and take calculator from daughter's hand. 2.9605263 it read. Ms Puss fingertip back her child's sandy hair: only adult teeth grinning from girl's mouth now: last baby tooth out three years ago.

Meow point to the calculator: "That number, it's how many times older than me you are. It's funny, isn't it?"

"That's right, Meow. It's funny."

Ms Puss push blue teddy bear closer to Meow's shoulder, then remember that a boyfriend gave it to her. Blue a stupid color for Teddy Bear—why not brown or black? Ms Puss breathe in and walk to window to watch traffic below. It scumbling everywhere, blurring road signs on all sides of hospital, like wandering trolls holding dancing seige. There and there, and going where? No escaping it, even in a dinky, all-American Alabama town.

"Then how come you're not laughing, Mom?"

"Oh baby, I am, I am." And Ms Puss's shoulders, they even shake to prove it.

Plant-moving

After Carpenterville bossman die of heart attack, killer company from stir-fry Japan buy everything, change name to HowYouSayIt Electronics, and promise Summons County it going to hire 200 more good American inhabitants to make computer parts. Japaneser come in, interview Oldcat—first time in life interviewer not know Oldcat's name from college football past, and this make him feel . . . him unsure just how and what it make him feel. Old? Confident in the new management? Uncirculated, like a collector's shiny copper penny? Whatever, super promotion which interviewer later congratulate him on make him feel great, that for certain.

New owners decide present plant too small and must build new one one mile away. Soon everyone in Carpenterville, not just Oldcat, seeing dollar signs.

"Soon we have twin-bill theater downtown."

"Soon we have discount U-pack-em grocery store."

"Soon we have real Mall."

"Soon we have K-Mart and Wal-Mart both."

Nine months later, plant-moving week come, and all employees loading boxes on trucks, so on and so forth. On second day, young black man get caught stealing color TV. This annoy Oldcat terrible because owners already discount TV's to actual cost for employees and rumor say owners going to give big plant-moving bonus for X-mas. Considering Mr Pick-him-nose who own plant before, this like Santa trade in rusty sleigh with missing floorboard and gutshot reindeer for wide-bottomed sampan and two polished bamboo oars.

Young man taken to local jail, while Oldcat and three other coat-and-ties meet in office that afternoon with Japanese president.

"My father and your all father frought one anothrel in Word Warl Two," president say, forming his own linguistic combat zone between Southern American and Japanese. "Stearing rike this no happen to their countries then."

No, they too busy killing one another to find time to steal, Oldcat think, remembering his Civil War buff father who sure enough fought in World War II, though in Africa, Sicily and Germany, not in the Pacific Islands.

Japanese president continue. "When my father and your all father . . ."

Oldcat always suspicious of good-old-day speeches. In good old days we take stupid young nigra and lynch him for TV theft until tongue hang out like left half of rabbit ears. In good old days we bomb Pearl Harbor and ally with Hitler. In good old days we drop atomic bombs on Hiroshima and Nagasaki—that no doubt cut down right fast on urban theft. Oldcat watch Japanese president, who in early fifties: him certainly not have eyes like Oldcat's father, nor cheekbones, nor lips—but something—what? Ah, bean sprout of gray arching over temple, just like Oldcat remember wafting along his father's cranium as it pored over old Civil War maps, stamps, and leaden bullets.

President talking, Oldcat half-listening.

"Probrem with Amerlica is you have too many bracks . . ."

Oldcat glance around: two coat-and-ties nodding sympathetically, only one raise eyebrows. Sometime Oldcat think if he brack he riot and steal just on general principle, after hearing trash like this. Japanese president finish by offering three solutions to theft problem—none, fortunately, involving a lynch mob. All white American coat-and-ties nod, then leave.

Just before quitting time that evening, a black man grab Oldcat's arm. It Ray Williams, who Oldcat soon learn is father of young man who steal TV. Ray Williams, who worked on the line that Oldcat supervised when he first came to Carpenterville and Alabama plant. Ray Williams, whose wife Little Bit gave young bachelor Oldcat more food than he could ever eat the first year he was here.

"As soon as that boy 'gan into high school, he fell in with bad trouble," Ray say. Oldcat study Ray's thin frame, his deep set eyes stirring semi-sweet chocolate. "He stop going to church and start drinking in sin. Little Bit and me is sorry 'bout him to the soles of our feet. I don't know what happen to some chirren today. Our girl, she fine, but the boy done gone to Satan. Some boys, they just born to meanness. Just born to it, no matter what their parents do."

Oldcat nod and reassure Ray, who one of best workers he ever had.

That evening, Oldcat stand alone in shiny hallway of plant. They ahead of schedule—this seem typical for Japanese across country, but Oldcat especially marvel that they able to accomplish the same in the Deep South—not always going to work, him bet. He think of Ray's son, no doubt now in Summons County jail, which have large chain link cage and basketball court wherein prisoners shoot hoops and dream themselves into Nike shoes before cheering crowds instead of near small highway before glaring racist eyes. Oldcat think of self after last back injury in college football—there come over a year where he drink heavy, get let off two DUI charges, start fights, and shoplift a gold ring. Fortunate that him not caught on last, or him never be big-time executive here at HowYouSayIt now.

Oldcat get in car and drive home, taking odd route by Summons County jail. Maybe, he think, the boy just need a talking to, maybe someone to show kindness and bail him out.

Sure enough, several men outside playing basketball in summertime dusk. Oldcat slow so that traffic light catch him and he can watch. Ray's son not playing ball; he making deal with someone standing outside the fence for what look like a pack of cigarettes—security never been rock-tight in Summons County jail. Of sudden, basketball thwunk fence. Ray's son not kick it polite-like back to players, but away into far corner. Oldcat have window down and can hear players curse. Ray's son turn around and flip them a finger, then shout, "What's your trouble, niggers?" Then he turn and see Oldcat staring and flip him a finger too, shout out, "What's your trouble, cracker?"

Deputy, he stand from chair and blow whistle just as basketball players getting ready to form circle and pound on some flesh.

"Stick that whistle up your ass. I don't need no save-me help with these trifling niggers."

And he been this way since starting high school? Brrr, Oldcat think. *Maybe they swap children in hospital on poor Ray and Little Bit.*

Horn blow from car behind, and Oldcat notice that the traffic light turn green. He drive straight, passing jail just like he in a Monopoly game. After all, it just plant-moving week, not world-moving. United Van Line and Mayflower both not be able to do that young man any good.

Edifice Complex

Oldcat been bringing in big money—for Summons County, Alabama, anyway—for over a year when he and Ms Puss decide to buy new home. Whatfor and whyto? They birth new set of twins? Open wayward orphanage? Adopt litter of kittens? No, none of these reasons. The words "new home" just spoken one day and like a magical wand woozily waved, Ms Puss and Oldcat bitten with new-house bug. You looking for reasons, you may as well read up in Oldcat's college engineering textbooks: he be moving soon, so he loan you one.

New Home: Oldcat and Ms Puss begin to scurry at those words like country roaches abandoning weathered shotgun shack upon spotting glossy Dolly Madison Cake truck repairing tire on two-lane out front. But though Oldcat and Ms Puss put out plenty nails and tacks, no stray cake truck pass. You see, it not as if Oldcat and Ms Puss can ride around mini-opolis of Carpenterville for weeks looking at houses for sale, or even broken-down cake trucks for rent. In fact, in only two and half day they see nearly everything that three and a half town realtors have to offer. Jesus, he spent more time shopping in Limbo, Oldcat say in especially blasphemous, anti-Catholic mood. Ms Puss just scowl and drag them to another home.

"Not big enough," Ms Puss whisper to Oldcat in that home.

"No upstairs," Oldcat whisper to Ms Puss in another.

"No this, no that," they chant.

Finally, friend Tom tell them about land for sale on other side of river, across from where he live in parents' old home. It on three acres and never been flooded, he tell them. And moresomeover, by just buying a lot they can design their own home with all the this's and that's they could ever need.

This this smell sweet as cream-filling in Dolly Madison cake to Oldcat and Ms Puss, so they drive with Tom to view land, the back acreage of which reach to the Sucarnochee River and belong to local farmer who forage cattle on it.

"Ever now and then, you'll get a good country whiff from those cattle," Tom say, laughing.

"I bet they're snakes out there!" Grrr shout, eyeing the field.

"I bet we can swing branch-to-branch all the way across the yard with so many trees!" Meow shout, keeping her eyes closer to what would be home.

Ms Puss mother-worry for a moment about both snakes and trees, but land so beautiful and her heart shout *Yes* so loudly that she just smile and agree. "Can we walk down to the river?" she ask.

"Sure," Tom answer. "Old man Reese won't mind. He's who you'd be buying this land from."

Since it early spring, the meadow grass not tall at all, and violet thistles just popping their heads like colorful faeries rising from some water underworld. Grrr kick at flowering violet of three-four these thistles before Ms Puss get mad:

"They so pretty, what you do that for, Grrr? Stop your meanness."

"Cows!" Meow yell, saving twin brother by pointing to a separate pasture. They all look to see black-and-white, brown-and-white faces munching last of winter rye grass. Grrr take aim at another thistle, but stop when Ms Puss take aim at him.

"Imagine waking up to that everyday," Oldcat sing, breathing in the mildly mooed air.

They nearly to river now, and can hear water. Sincetime Oldcat been living in Carpenterville, this river never flood—that of course not mean that it *never* flood, so he ask Tom.

"I've seen it happen twice: once it ran up over the bridge over there and tore down part of our back porch—that was when I was a kid about Grrr and Meow's age, and that was the worst. That time it got just about to that black walnut tree on the rear of your three acres here. The other time, it came to the bottom of the bridge and didn't bother much else."

"Where's your house, Tom?" Ms Puss ask.

"You can see it now, right at the end, near the bridge." Tom point a pudgy finger. "See that dark red wood siding? In summertime, you won't be able to spot it for all the trees. My parents loved trees of all kinds, so we've got a forest on six acres. I helped plant a lot of them."

"You mean you've lived in the same house since you were a kid?" Meow ask this with wonder at such piddling pedestrian poverty.

"We've already lived in two," Grrr adds, proud of the fact and jutting his jaw.

"I know that. I helped you move into both of them, didn't I? The first one was when you two were still little surprises inside your mother's tummy."

Both Grrr and Meow look to their mother. A five-foot log is floating lazily downriver, and Ms Puss walks toward it to hide her blushing.

"The worst flood we had—the one when I was a kid—carried two telephone poles and a car down into the bridge over there," Tom adds, picking up on lost subject. His eyes glim somewhere distant, like he starring in some lonesome B + W movie.

"Was anyone in the car?" Grrr asks, sniffing the air.

"Grrr!" Ms Puss admonish, turning around. "What a question!"

"Yeah, in fact there was."

Tom pause for a moment to let Grrr's eyes return from turnip-size, and Oldcat can tell Tom's rearranging some part of the story. Tom's parents were killed in a car accident, but that was in Florida, when Tom was in junior college, so Oldcat wonders why he's making up something now. To keep Grrr and Meow innocent? To save some neighbor from scandal? Secrets, they nearly everywhere in small town, like glaze-eyed rats nibbling in corn bin.

"There were two old farmers," Tom says, starching his story in his mind. "Their car had driven off a small upriver bridge in all the rain, and they weren't able to get out. Me and my dad found them and called the sheriff."

"What'd they look like? All wrinkled up?" Grrr ask.

"Grrr!" Ms Puss yell.

Listening to this story make the first time that it occur to Oldcat that he might spend rest of life in Carpenterville, be buried in local cemetery, have grandchildren raised in same town, same cow pasture. That him too might keep glaze-eyed secrets nibbling at hard corn. Well, doing so not hurt Tom. But then, it sure chew the kernel-soul out of some of these local full-of-hate tobacco-breaths. . . .

"Mr. Tom, how come you're not moving into a new house?" Meow asks, resuming her previous line of thought.

"Cause I live by myself. There's no need for a new house."

"How come you don't get married then, like Mom and Dad?"

"Cause I'm waiting for you to get old enough, beautiful."

Meow giggle at that. The log Ms Puss been watching now caught on a snag about twenty yards up. It bob, churning foam. Ms Puss once commented to Oldcat that she thought Tom was still getting over his parents' death, that *that* was why he didn't marry. She'd been reading self-help books then, stacking them upwards like castle walls and always talking about unresolved childhood problems gurgling like dank moats. She'd also then been trying to get Tom and her friend Jackie Babe hitched, but according to Ms Puss, Jackie Babe harbored a lot of unresolved childhood problems too, so hitching post stay mostly mired far out in dark, swampy woods.

All that make Oldcat smile now. Unresolved problems, like the Edifice Complex. He wonder if he and Ms Puss warped by some deep-seated unresolved childhood problem—maybe they fell from a treehouse, or maybe they tried to toddle away and live in a doghouse but only got a spanking and eight huge flea bites—maybe that come why they never satisfied with where they live.

"I want a house like Uncle Tom's," Grrr say, hurling a rock at the bobbing log. "I want a house with stilts too."

"We could do that," Oldcat speak, half aloud. And when Ms Puss raise her eyebrows at him, he explain, "We could. We could build a balcony off our bedroom or the kitchen. See in those sweetgums where the hill slopes over—"

"Neat!" Grrr and Meow shout, proving themselves truly twins from same womb, same day.

Oldcat stare toward the three acres that he already know they going to buy. Him envision house in middle of all those just budding sweetgums, maybe a sudden inexplicable deep South snowstorm blowing off the new house rooftop and balcony. And there! Yes, there he stand with family, happy and settled at last. He raise his hand and wave discreetly to self, to Ms Puss and twins who standing on future balcony watching future out-of-character snowstorm. *You going to stay put, or Edifice Complex going to uproot you again?* he mouth to future self gaping at uncommon future weather. But that self refuse to answer, pretending it not even see him, it just run hand through own whiskers and grin, place arm around twins, then stare downriver, where some log bobbing, like leaves astir in some gargantuan fortune-teller's fragile cup of oolong tea.

So Old

Ms Puss, she mad at Oldcat. He layabout Football Monday Nite with Tomboys (so supposed said he so) at Oysterhead Lounge one too many time. She been to Oysterhead with dirty-girl, once-friend, quick-divorcee Jackie. Perfume, smoke, no lights, and booze mix lurky selves into hubba-hubba magic Ms Puss know all too well. Ms Puss at kitchen door thinking about this, watching river flow, and Ms Puss know that mindsome activity bode no good.

. . . So, when Oldcat drive home that night, when he scrape lamppost, mumble him fix tomorrow, when she say Meow call asking for more college money and him not even react, just slosh to bedroom like he a catfish and try humpy-hump with her, she say:

"What matter? I suppose you no get none nonny from Jackie Sweets."

When all this happen, he stop like iceberg surveying river entry, finding it much too small.

"Whatworld make you say that?" he ask.

But him stop Einsteinian millisecond-fraction too long before he speak, so Ms Puss no answer his stupid question, she just turn away and shoulder-shake cry all night. There: *that* what thinking get a person. How Einstein ever stand it?

Now she up Tuesday morning, washing already washed dishes in already clean sink. Her open wrong cupboard, spot Drain-o. That sight start her big wish list:

1. Oldcat drunk-snore, Drain-o down throat she pour? No.

2. Oldcat drunk lay, Liquid Plum-R on penis she spray? No.

3. She telephone Jackie Sweets? "Jackie Babe. Long time, no see. You come over for brunch, pop Dom Perignon like old times?" Jackie Sweets come, Ms Puss lead her into bedroom, show Oldcat sprawled in drunk-snore. "There, Jackie. You want, you take. There's a big red wheelbarrow out back." No, not that one either.

4. Call lawyer-cat who once climb apple tree for Ms Puss in another

county, another time? Flirt? (Oooh, how So-Big-and-Handsome-Tree-Cat still you are. You take me and divorce case under wing, burn Oldcat in courtroom of adultery hell?) No, she not do that either.

5. What about wrap self in blue cellophane, play Turkish music and greet Oldcat at door every night? But what then will neighbors say? Will children then ever come home from college to visit? Ever bring prospective husband, wife to see nymphomaniac mother?

6. What about play Tammy Wynette loud enough that all Summons County hear "Stumble by Your Man" and feel so sorry for her they pray and eat commemorative fried chicken drumsticks in umpteen churches? Or what about start drinking Old Crow? Agh. I not sure which leave worse taste in mouth, drumstick grease or whiskey.

7. Could maybe move out on cattle ranch with crazed lean uncle, watch every young and old thing in Marengo County waltz around him and cow paddies. Agh, Jackie Babe always have crush on uncle, she probably show up and I have to pull shotgun down from fireplace.

8. What left then? Do nothing? Yes, yes, yes. Do nothing, stop thinking, watch river.

Yes? Yes? Yes? Stop thinking? *Oh Ms Puss, Ms Puss,* she hear self moan while opening dolphin-free tuna can—*how you ever get so old?*

Wednesdays

Doing Own Thing

Yes, it so: Oldcat, him like a good politician: him only spearmint with drug in college, and here's how it happened:

At frat-jock party when him vying for king of drunken get-crazy hill, his new, pretty-tit Ft. Lauderdale girlfriend who just as dumb as he, goat him on: "Little town boy from Kentucky 'fraid of big city life?"

It not like, after all, Gainesville, Florida really big city, but noneless, him smoke a joint to make city girl happy and prove he a man. *Hack-hack, duuuuuhhh.* That consist of his total experience. This the promised big city? he wonder while he wait for drug to go away.

Now some pablums will tell you pot good, that it create no more harm than silly dare or joke, lot less than alcohol or tobacco smoke. Maybe so for them, but after Oldcat watch this girlfriend slip one night, two night, three night and more down marijuana's slippery slope, him never again believe in pot of gold. These all the happens in four months that happen:

1. She quit physics class. "It stupid."

2. She laugh at all her singing sorority sisters that had been her friend. "Them stupid."

3. She listen only to tiny tape and record collection, she watch only tiny b + w TV. "Want to go out?" Oldcat ask. "Canoe down Sewanee River? Party at Tim's? Shop at mall?" / "No," she manage to whisper, her voice cracking like dry barn board curing in hot Florida sun, "No, them all stupid." Then she turn music low, raise sound on sitcom TV; shake head, turn TV low, music up; shake head, repeat, repeat. She testing speakers, Oldcat wonder. Or ears? Or sanity?

4. She quit sorority, sorority quit her?

5. Same ditto-like with college.

6. Her get apartment. "Woo-hoo," Oldcat chant to jock friends, licking lip, buying big box prophylactic. "I soon go jumpity-bump until little Oldcat, him get red-eye sore and squawk surrender." But little Oldcat no have chance, cause big Oldcat forget about girlfriend's tiny tape, tiny record, and b + w TV: "Oldcat, listen to this so-sad 'Bridge Over Troubled Water' song. Don't Simon and Garfunkel just make you want to die? Oldcat, stop that! stop that! Let's look at this funny funny Saturday Nite Live rerun."

Stop, listen, look. Oldcat hear this so much that he think he dating a train.

And the list of bad happenings just go on and grow:

7. "Parents stupid," she say when they no send no more money.

8. Her get waitress job in fancy steak house. Her big tits go away. Wherever to? Oldcat wonder. Marijuana smoke dry them up? That possible? And though she a waitress, she no wear make-up anymore. "Make-up stupid."

9. Her no longer smile when she see Oldcat. Her just look, like glaze-eyed hen hatching an egg. Oldcat worry: Eggshell, it going to break open soon? "Want to smoke a J?" she ask, giving first big grin of night. Oldcat, him shake head. Last time him smoke with her, him cough all next day during windsprints. Though him explain reason, his refusal upset girlfriend, make her worry he a narc or something worse—Southern Baptist maybe, she joke. Her dark eyes so serious, though, that Oldcat forget to laugh.

10. Her lose waitress job in fancy restaurant, get another in pizza house. She and Oldcat fight, she scream: "My pizza boss is stupid, college is stupid, your sport team's stupid, politics is stupid, born-again religion's stupid, this hick Florida town's stupid, you're stupid!" That Sermon on Mount finished, they go to bed and screw. "Screwing's stupid," she laugh, head smothered in pillow of tears.

11. Oldcat not know what to do. Him call, she no answer. Him believe she probably not hear phone cause she smoke pot and listen to record, tape, TV—all at same time.

"She's doing her own thing," friend advise.

"Yes," Oldcat answer.

But him wonder, as him drive by time and time to see new sad-eyed, hippie supposed friends smoking J's on front porch—yes, him wonder: she doing own thing, or thing, it doing her?

Southern Lights

Where this come from? Some Alaskan open his refrigerator?

Oldcat and Ms Puss stand on elevated deck outside new house and stare at snow falling in night sky, drifting down dandruff clumps as thick as old man Reese's. Just the few minutes they been spent outside kitchen back door, one inch, maybe more, float to ground.

"We should get the kids up—obviously there won't be school tomorrow," Ms Puss say.

"Probably learn more from a snowstorm than they would from Summons County Academy anyway."

Ms Puss stand amid falling snowflakes and twist toward her husband, start to say something, but only shake her head as an oversize snowflake nuzzles into her ear. This sorry point about racist academy schooling been a cold thorn that little citizens Ms Puss and Oldcat yet unable to resolve, so they both just raise eyebrows and walk inside, changing subject to happier news:

"Grrr? Meow? It's snowing outside. Come on, get up."

"Snow! ?xo*%!!"

Snow, that secret, almost foreign word to deep Southern vocabulary, gargle comic book exclamations through both children's throats, and they immediate bang foreheads to window and, "Wow!"

Soon dressed and outside they are, jumping on deck that overlook old man Reese's field and cattle.

"Where're the cows, Mom?" Meow ask. "Aren't they going to catch cold?"

"That one I defer to you, Mr Dad."

Oldcat been busy staring open-mouthed at sky dropping snow like D-Day parachutists in old war film, so question have to be re-stated. On hearing it again, he look down and see long, empty field and wonder himself about cows. But it really not all that cold. Him remember from living in Kentucky that it never supposed to be really cold when it snow—at least that what Kentuckians say—maybe Alaskans or Canadians or even New Yorkers say different.

"They lying warm in shed," he finally answer, making his own lying. "Besides, they've got thick leather coats they wear, yes?"

"Then how come they're not too hot in the summer?" Grrr retaliate.

Ms Puss scoop a snowball from along deck's railing and throw it at Grrr, once more saving day—or night so be this case—for her mate, who not exactly a Mr Greenjeans, despite engineering degree.

"&*#@!" Grrr and Meow scream on feeling their first snowball and rushing down steps. Soon enough, parents join in apple tree backyward with comic book language of their own.

"(*^@$%!)*&&!"

"You better not say that again, Mr Know-it-all!"

"(*^@$%!)*&&!"

When Oldcat say this, Ms Puss let him collect snowball right on his cranium, rattling seven, maybe eight thousand precious of his electronic engineering brain cells. Well, he think, there go last possibility of Nobel Prize for second best picture tube ever, so he compress snow in hand and retaliate against wife.

"Let's walk down toward the river," Meow shout after they finish snowball fight.

"Snakes!" Grrr yell.

"It's too cold for snakes, honey," Ms Puss laugh. Don't need to be even Mrs—or Ms—Greenjeans to figure that one out.

And so they walk, hearing wind lapping across the field amid the bleat of snow-crushed wildflowers that have been blooming for nearly a week. Most time when it snow, Oldcat remember from Kentucky, it very quiet, but this night clank loud with trees cracking under the weight of the wet snow falling so fast, their budding branches caught off guard by this late spring winter storm invading the Deep South.

"Instead of burning cities, this snow going to freeze them. Not Sherm 'em, but Shiver 'em," Oldcat comment.

Grrr and Meow stop and look at father in getting-white dark. "Huh?" they both ask, trying to see his face.

"Sherman, as in General and Yankee. What you no doubt supposed to learn in sch—"

"Oldcat!" Ms Puss yell in warning. "Don't bring up that subject, don't spoil this beautiful snow."

A large branch drop with a terrible crash on the other side of the river, and Oldcat wonder about his friend Tom who live in his parent's old house over there. Oldcat look, but no can see a thing except millions of flakes of snow. He sigh, for they so like tiny pure souls searching for shelter, swept homeless up and down the land by tall wind shrieking heartlessly, like smug S & L board of directors cackling over Courvoissier.

Of sudden, behind, street lights go out and a loud thwack echo through the air. Oldcat and family turn to see a violet ball glowing over their neighbor's house. "That must be the transformer," Oldcat say.

Not no sooner does he say his say when another violet ball burst to the east, over the river. Then another, high in the sky. Then all three disappear into swirling white-black night.

"Consider my last Mr Know-it-all statement inoperative," he announce. Two more of the weird violet balls burst in the sky; the wind keeps pace by cracking more tree branches, almost in a rhythm; and the snowy souls keep falling, from who knows where.

"Northern lights? Lightning? What is it?" Ms Puss ask, taking Oldcat's arm.

"Spaceships!" Grrr shout.

Well, it not the transformer, anyway, Oldcat think, unsettled. But the adventure of snow pulls him onward, and he looks back at the sky to see that the streetlights are off all over town now, and off over the industrial park just south of them too, cause there not usual small city light refracting in the sky. "Maybe your dad will no work tomorrow and we can build a snowman when this snow gets wet from sunlight."

"What if the spacemen burn up the sun?"

"Space*WOMEN,*" Ms Puss say.

"SNOW-WOMAN!" Meow screech, adding her own zest to feminism.

"SpaceBUG! And we'll have a contest to see who can build the biggest, me and Dad, or you and Mom!" Grrr shouts, running through the snow, holding his arms out like a night owl swooping on prey. But when another violet light flashes and two trees near the river crack at same time, he runs close to Ms Puss, looking with big, spacebugged eyes.

"Is it safe out here, Oldcat?" Ms Puss ask.

Oldcat really not too sure of answer to that question, but him think as long as lightning just flashing up in clouds and not toward ground, as long as they keep in open field away from falling trees, they be okay. Besides, him haven't felt so alive and remembered so many childhood Kentucky scenes in years. Tobacco sales in autumn, horse sales in spring, bluegrass and bumblebees in summer. And in winter, he used to love plodding through snowdrifts around parents' house; he used to trudge round neighborhood and shovel off walks for one dollar-fifty apiece. Oh yes, big businessman—if only he'd invested in stocks, not *Uncle Scrooge* comic books, he'd be retired today.

They're near the river now, he can hear it flowing, see its black bank. Some quarter mile downstream is Tom's house: his lights are off too, but he's probably safely beer-dreaming of some long ago war or philosopher-king anyway, Oldcat think.

The whole family stops and huddles on the bank, in a clearing away from any trees. Snowflakes keep falling in the water and dissolving, to contrast with the cottony accumulation on the river's bank. Oldcat stares as Grrr and Meow throw, into the rushing water, snowballs whose pure white heads bob not even once, just disappear, like they too of the myriad, multiple, and many homeless. *Why you thinking this homeless stuff, anyway,* Oldcat ask self. It a good thing it no snow every winter night down Deep South, or you be strapped in bed, on anti-compressant or worse.

"Let's move back some," Ms Puss say, tugging Oldcat's arm. "We're too near falling trees. I like the field better."

Oldcat nod, wondering if she can see his little chin and beard shivering in the glare of the snow against the night.

After one more snowball fight they go back to their house, to find that of course the electric heat off too, so Oldcat start a fire in the fireplace while Ms Puss move bedsheets, pillows and blankets to living room floor.

"This is just like cavemen," Grrr say when all snuggled in makeshift bed together. "Are we going to get up early tomorrow and kill a sabertooth tiger, Dad?"

"CaveWOMEN," Meow laugh.

"You bet," Oldcat answer, forgetting the homeless on feeling daughter's warm flannel nightshirt rub his elbow. "Tomorrow, we all four chew Red Man and trap a bear."

Meow squirm and Ms Puss make mock retching sound, but for that mystic Southern Lights moment in that mystic Southern Lights night, they all four fall asleep imagining whatever so they want, that being best education available anyway.

Biology Lab

Ms Puss, when returning as adult nursing student in local junior college, sit in cafeterium semi-minding own business, watching lungeous professor and giggled co-ed at nearby table. Professor, his white, pure hands carefully pull out essay; coed look at grade thereonupon and giggles disappear, replaced by downspout pout like hometown doll factory been H-bombed.

Ms Puss, she so bored with reproductive biology of paramecium that she shut text and listen. Yak-yak, yipple-yip about coed's lousy humanities paper, then surprise-o! Still sniffling student conduct her own interview of professor, evidently canvassing for slumming sociology class: "Question One: How long have you taught? Are you married? How many children have you and your wife had? Question Two: How many times have you taught this same course? How many times have you taught from this same book? Question Three: Do you and your wife own your own home? Are you planning on retiring? Are you looking forward to it?"

My lordgoodgod, Ms Puss think, this young she soon drop professor into grave while Jell-o in his fingernails still growing, dandruff from his hair still falling. Ms Puss lean to hear more, hoping noseybody cafeterium chair not creak and give her away. She think she spy gray tomb moss already formate on professor's whiskers, even as the young she babble on. Then Ms Puss notice that professor, he too leaning, but he staring at student's forehead while she talk. What so interesting there? Certainly not brain.

Ms Puss tower-of-Pisa some more, sniff perfume (an expensive eau du snoot), watch coed's foot jerk-a-lerk a Gucci shoe, watch her butt twist a Bugle Boy patch, see her blouse frimple an Anne Taylor tag, her sweater sway one by Calvin Klein—and conclude that this girl a business major who volunteer entire body as class project for America's 1st mobile designer tag display unit. Ultimate idea no doubt to renovate discarded mobile-home libraries, showcase instead underage nubiles with temporary licenses driving through traffic lights, parading latest bras, jock straps, and panties.

But professor live in dandruffed clouds, too dowdy to know Calvin Klein from Miss Erika or Miss Piggy, so labels certainly not what he leaning so thresholdly to see . . . ah, Ms Puss discern the mystery and barely stifle a giggle.

Can it truly be? Yes, centimetering across coed's forehead like paramecium escaped from biology text trips a tiny white crab, better known as *crabbus grabbus.* Professor, he blink as girl obliviumly ask sociology survey question number four. He look like he want to itch his own forehead, but not dare. Ms Puss see him stop his right hand by gripping table as he answer question instead and somehow not laugh.

That right, Teach, Ms Puss want to say, *You can read 'em and write 'em and even dress 'em up, but you can't take 'em out.* She shove her biology book aside, cause this all scene more informative than cutting on kidnapped neighborhood cat in sterile laboratory anyoldway.

Ms Puss's only regret as lunchtime show continue with questions five and six? She regret she not trained as a fine seamstress so she could quick-stitch a tiny hot-pink teddy for the luminescent body crab edging along coed's pretty blonde hairline. That way, the two form the perfect mobile designer label pair.

Fortune

Oldcat one time have Kentucky friend who own a bar. Everybody be that friend's friend. To the left of him, to the right of him—like sailor on driftwood surrounded by saltwater, that friend surrounded by friends.

And too, him make money paw over claw, spend it like footloose racehorse at Keeneland racetrack purchasing fresh spring hay: "You need drink? Here, let me buy. Your friend too? Okey-dokey. Hey stranger, what about you?"

Yes, friend original Digger teleported straight from 17th century, though him no wear black or preach, or even carry tambourine. (Foreshadowy hint: Too bad this friend not at least wear uniform and incorporate self like The Salvation Army. That way when Wheel of . . .)

Yes, Wheel of Fortune do give its ha-ha jokester tumble and friend and business partner argue, so friend's bar sold one day. Now Oldcat's friend have more money than him in life ever have. If whoo-hoo party before, whee-hee party now. Friend's friends expand like they nimble limbs on square root tree. Do friend ever slow to think, *Ahh, Fortuna, Fortuna, how like WD-40 your wheel doth roll? You hold, no doubt, something else in store for me?* No, he just rise like sun, which never fret about when it gonna set. After all, him may not be original digger or even smart book-learned existentialist, but who counts rice when wading in the paddy? And who counts money when it hidden in the bank?

Bankers. That answer that last dumb question.

Of consequent, Wheel of Fortune give both checking account and safety vault two loud thwacks. This noise, Oldcat and you might think, slow friend down. No. Him remain faithful to rice paddy rules: breathe, eat, drink whiskey, and be merry as . . .

Friend's friends, though, they let go when big Fortune wheel start churning downhill; otherwise they tear their flimsy arms, no? Yes. Of consequent, friend's friends become like coontails on car antennae: that is, to existential no more.

Oldcat hear rumors beading down I-75 like hot axle grease and hence decide to from past visit. Friend have become hermit in cold wintery brick house, and promise to show Oldcat a treasure after few social drinks. Treasure? Oldcat study bare walls of brick, which cast back dark blood-red silhouettes from another century. See, this back in Lexington, Kentucky, and Sherman not burn that compromised town. So, did friend discover Civil War stash? Original diary of Mary Todd Lincoln? Oldcat pace inside of house, sip Bardstown bourbon, examine chinks in brick walls and drool. What ghostly treasure could be hoo-ooing other than cold wind through cracked windows and stained blinds? Hidden Confederate stamps worth millions? Gold bars secreted away before closing of Fort Knox? "One more drink, then you see, Oldcat."

Oldcat by now wary. This been three strong whiskey drinks and him have looked around dumpy house long enough to wonder maybe if this stash be hoard of Monopoly money ferreted from city trash. Or maybe it a cache of old hair dryers that friend collect from neighborhood garbage cans for to re-sell copper wiring.

"Here! Here they are!" friend at last say, bringing out wirebound notebook of poems embellished with chicken grease and white bread crumbs. Oldcat, frantic on seeing poem-words scratched on greasy paper, search about room for antique treasures tucked away. But no, these poems, these poems, these poems. . . . Quick! What about under lumpy couch where friend now sit, Oldcat think with sudden vision. But no, these poems, these poems. . . . What about in empty fireplace that friend too poor to light? No, these poems, these poems. . . .

Oldcat sink in squeaking chair and read, not too polite-like, either.

Where treasure, where fortune? Him eyes keep oozing that question.

Where it be? These poems, they nothing. In desperation, Oldcat read, search deep between lines just like he in freshman English all over again, even try reading lines backwards, hoping some treasure map hidden in Hebraic code. Nothing appear. Where fortune could be hid?

Fortune? Ahh, open eyes, stupid, stupid Oldcat. Want to know where fortune lies? This entire room and city could dwindle to lead but the Golden Rule would still remain alchemical and golden. Dig, digger, and be a better friend. Look up from traitorous words. Look up at smiling red face sitting on lumpy couch directly before you. Look, cause he who have charitable eyes can always see to see.

Fame

Oldcat, when working at pizza parlor, be the youngest pizza cook in nation to brush with fame. No, him not meet Papa Luigi; no, him not expose Mafia wash 'em money ring; no, him not on cover of *TIME* to flip pizza, health food of future, in secretly ozoning air. Even better than all these at once: him meet actual first cousin of Mytch Ryder and the Detroit Wheels.

You no know Mytch Ryder?

What, then, you know about fame?

By the Dawn's Early Light

Oldcat, after promotion, him have all: BigMouseWerke car, Yap-a-knees motorcycle, two cellular phones, one yahoozie. Him eat newblown cuisine. Pretty Burmese cat him have, plus many plastic credit cards. Him have tape-on-tape, continuous digital play. Him have Big Screen. Him have fax and modem. Him have CD player and seventeen tweetery speakers in BigMouseWerke car. Him have home computer to file, alphabetize, systematize, enumerate, regurgitate many catalogues and fiber optic shopping lists.

One morning, from one on-line catalogue, a bright gold glint catch Oldcat's eye just like he Howard Carter peeking at mummy of baby king Tut. "Wonderful things. I see wonderful things."

So him order Rolex. Meanwhile, him finger expensive silver coin collection that keep him busy electronic bulletinboarding on computer and modem; him polish three Martin guitars but never play; him flop-drop oversize books on coffee table but never read; him oil four shotgun, three .22, six antique pistoles but never shoot. Not enough! Back to computer to order Monopoly board made of platinum and subscribe to *Smithsonian, Scientific American, Atlantic, Good Housekeeping, New Yorker,* and . . . and since on-line go temp off-line and since him heart pound from fingertips performing so many walkings, him legs demand equal time. They shuffle him to polish Martin guitar on wall, re-arrange pretty picture books on table, ogle computer fish swimming to save him computer screen from burnout. One fish glow like soon-to-get Rolex. Stomp your foot madly, Oldcat! Ask, *When it come?* O mailman, O mailwoman (Oldcat, you no care which) just bring the thing. Bring the thing! Bring the thing! Bring! Thing! Bring! Thing!

Oldcat shake like delirium tremens and clatter imported African beewswax guitar polish onto Italian marble tabletop to run, for computer catalogue now back on Pentium on-line: *America, America, On-line shed its grace on thee!* Leaning very close to low radiation screen until him whiskers catch static, he spy jade head of Nefertiti from Metropolitan Museum of Art and him notice it cost only 495 dollar on credit card, shipping free.

Buy! Buy! Buy!

Buy!

Buy-buy.

What is it him not notice in his frantic finger's war dance? Ahh, him not notice own wife and teenage twins standing by, slack-mouthed and dismayed in other room; him not notice own expensively capped teeth glinting in low radiation screen like drunken American sailor's cap loudly revelling just before dawn, Pearl Harbor Day.

My Most Memorable Character

Oldcat work one college summer in a newspaper pressroom, despite sportball doctor's orders. Oldcat about to give up on doctor anyway, who prognose that him busted back never again football will play. Him about to give up on football too, though him not know it in big livingroom of mind yet. And girlfriend, she done flown coop, a scrawny bird busily pecking marijuana seeds. In such inbetweenland, he work and grab newspaper bundles from ughsome gray strapping machine, stack them on pallet for ughsome yellow forklift to haul outside—all while saving pink fingers from machine's evil cutting blade that chop decisive and direct, like from b+w gangster movie.

Yes, tie even Humphrey Bogart under that gray whanger and after just one finger's worth of blood sampling, him sing louder than any Maltese falcon could ever scree.

Only reason Oldcat persist in clocking body in on time card is because of brain's secret hope that this grunting and lifting will cure broke back just like constant weightlifting, and since him barred from university's weight room because of same stupid doctor . . . well, do please, dear body, clock in. Spine and fingers, however, not so sure that doctor's prognosis not right. And ears, they live in absolute panic because of WHUMPA-WHUMPA-WHUMPA pressroom noise forever shaking the twelve-inch reinforced concrete floor. How we ever going to hear quarterback sneak even suppose broke back does get cured, they wail out to brain. You and silly axon-neurons enclosed in thick skull, so you okay; but stop to consider rest of body.

But all brain hear is WHUMPA-WHUMPA, which it somehow translate to Hut-hut-four, hike-the-ball-and-out-the-door.

Second month at job, a skinny named Mark is hired to work on other gray strapping machine. On their third buddy-buddy session, on their third magical beer after a special afternoon job, Mark inform Oldcat that he hail from Boston, where he mugged on MTA and have throat slashed one night when walking through turnstile.

"This lawyer walked into my hospital room a few days later and had me signing papers while I was still under sedation, so now I'm suing MTA for poor safety precautions. I didn't see the guy who mugged me at all. I was a little drunk when it happened, but I'm not supposed to tell anyone that, the lawyer says."

They two sit drinking beer in tiny rental trailer that Mark share with mysterium globular man who float about slick as congealing catfish oil in deep fry but who suppos-ed studying on Captain's license to sail freighter full of uranium ore and computer parts to Shang-hai or better. Just before sun set and fourth beer-tab pop, little next door trailer boy come ask for would-be Captain, who not there but out studying barnacle and plankton formations in local lounge, of which sea-worthy knowledge will no doubt help on license exam for captainancy.

Little white-face boy, on hearing this news, look up so penitent, as if ready to kneel and wail cherubic castrato sailor shanty in hope that his angelic voice will float the seaside air to entice Yo-ho Captain back from barnacle studies. But since there only three blades of St. Augustine grass growing out in trailer park, and since boy's knees already look skinned, he not kneel just whimper wide-eyed at Oldcat, turn tail and leave.

"What in the world that little kid want with—"

"Mind your own business," Mark briefly say.

Oldcat swallow and glance from boy's loose pants and pink bare feet padding away, to Mark's throat, where he can discern no slice-line from evil MTA mugger. Maybe is this because of fine plastic surgeon and rosy evening sky casting shadow? . . .

Mark continue with story he been telling: "I was in for six weeks. For a while, I panicked that the guy was going to break in and cut my throat again, like on TV, but they never caught him anyway. A plastic surgeon fixed my cut. A really good one. Then for six months after I got out, I was afraid to go anywhere in public, you know?"

"After you got out of . . ."

"The hospital, where else?"

Where else? How about dry-out tank, how about moss-bricked penitentiary, how about close-shuttered child abuse center, how about drinking Mad

Dog 20-20 in hot summer back of abandoned GoodWill truck—that where else.

This Mark, he one of those people who ooze bad luck like garlic from each and every of fifty thousand pores. Oldcat look around at yo-ho captain roommate's leftover girlie and muscle magazines littered everywhere, then stand up to retrieve beer from 'fridge.

"Toss me one," Mark say.

Oldcat do and Mark drop it to knock over lit cigarette and half full beer already beside him. Cigarette burn hole in carpet, beer drain onto today's mail. This all happen so natural that Mark not even bother to curse.

Late that summer, Oldcat quit both pressroom and dreams of football to return to University of Florida and study calculus squiggles in electronic engineering. But before he leave, he party with pressroom gang—Mark, Sarge and foxy bleach blonde line-inserter sporting green ribbon on arm—one last time. Though he miss all them, he hope never to see newspaper loading dock or pressroom again: this not because of him back or fingers, for they fine; it because of him ears, who both together feel they flown through 90 day bombing strike against Hanoi, only to have it magnetically replayed backwards on Watergate tape.

For six-seven month, Oldcat think of Mark every time he near dark street corner or turnstile. He try to call trailer for many rings; finally, newspaper say Mark quit, not even pick up last paycheck—maybe Mark win his MTA case and Boston lawyer squeeze off big settlement nest egg down Gainesville way. Oldcat figure if this so he meet Mark buying rounds in local bar. But no show.

So maybe bad luck Mark run into another turnstile visiting another city, or maybe he accidental arrested on roommate's child molestation charges. Maybe *both*; after all, Mark tell how he once bitten by five ground-rattlers when hunting doves and spend four day in hospital. Bad luck seem to follow Boston Strange-ler like skin follow most people.

. . . Eventually, time do its doodle thing and Mark disappear from Oldcat's brainpan like sludgy off-shore oil . . . to re-appear today, six years later when Oldcat working hump-day nightshift at Summons

Electronics and walk into men's bathroom at plant and notice two of three lights out, leaving men's stalls glimmering an ominous yellow. He stop, notice huge wad of unravelled toilet paper lurking under nearest yellow stall like killer's carefully discarded cotton glove.

Unzipping at urinal, Oldcat hear muffled cough out in hall and protectively grab throat, thinking of Mark. Funny thing, though: now he no longer sure whether to imagine Mark getting throat cut or Mark doing the cutting.

—Yeah, that about typical for a Florida character sketch, Oldcat realize, barely able to pee because he glancing so nervously at door and about, feeling Adam's apple tingle like it espy glinting straight razor unfolding to slice. Him can remember Civil War Buff dad always reading "My Most Memorable Character" aloud from *Reader's Digest* to improve son's morals. Him dad then leave them stacked around house like vitamin nuggets, until even mousie mom throw them away. Dad even try own luck and write character essay, but it never accepted. Oldcat remember seeing dad sadly open rejecting envelope—

—suddenly one of toilet stalls gurgle and Oldcat glance nervously at all the unflushed urinals and cigarette ashes. Eight urinals, and eleven of them unflushed. He look to stall, then realize it empty and that Summons County plumbing just entertaining self. It doing so with same ineffectual as himownmind?

You just gotta get out and meet a new crowd, he been telling that same mind for weeks, and now he realize it's true. What better day than humpday to make a change? *You just gotta get out, honest, find some friends. Just don't look for them in character essay or on the MTA.*

Nature Lover

Driving alone one sunny summer morning, Oldcat roll down window to *zazen* some crisp air like he see performed by bejewelled Seattle Zen Buddhist Monk on late-nite talk show. *One two three four five* etc., he count as he send all bad divorce thought into country air surrounding him. One! Him exhale thought of angry Ms Puss and pretty Jackie Babe; him reconsider, then exhale thought of pretty Miss Puss Babe and angry Jackie. Two! Him sigh out thought of traumatized broken-home teens Meow and Grrr. Three! Him huff out thought of alimony. Four! Him sniff out thought of disappointed Tom who played best man at wedding. Five! Him cough out thought of treacherous Jackie Babe who walked as bride's maid at same. Six! Him grip wheel and wheeze out thought of stupid father-in-law whom he like despite the both themselves. Seven! Him hack, between clenched lips, thought of slick lawyers making money off family misery. Eight! Him gargle out thought of name appearing in local newspaper's legal notices under big 'D' for divorce. Nine! Him murmur thought of one more American statistic of broken families playing like broken records. Ten! Him exhale—

—No! These sweetgum and sycamore trees too pretty for all that terrible pollution crap to spill out over them. Only jewels you have are two family ones dangling between legs.

So Oldcat, nature lover and original subconscious founder of Greenpeace, inhale in gargantual OM to pull it all back in. He even reverse car on deserted road to make sure. "Come back, Five! Come back, Four!" he shout outside window.

Zazen be damned, him think, inhaling last putrid puff and holding his breath. Be a man and face it, Oldcat. This rotting murk all belong to you anyway.

Art Appreciation

Teenaged Oldcat, him have tall friend who decide to wear white cowboy hat. This geography not in Texas or even Alabama ya-hoo, but in Kentucky Go-Blue. Friend don hat—no other goofy verb describe the silly head-gluing of his vanilla barrel, as tall as an Italian wedding cake, on his burr-topped head—he don it, and moresomeover, he decide to parade it in public after cooking half an evening at a pizzeria. "You look like walking museum of cowboy art," Oldcat tease. Friend flip Oldcat a finger, then go out.

Two Go Big Blue fans walking out from nearby lounge see hat, smell lanky mozzarella boy, and laugh.

"You laugh at my hat?" friend ask.

"You bet," both answer.

Do friend have dilemma? Do him have panic/flight reaction? Do him pretend ear stuffed with mozzarella and tomato sauce so thick that he not understand strangers? Do him even just smile and thank men for their friendly fashion column advice?

No way, for him say, "Then we going to fight."

Oldcat hear all this the next day and laugh so hard at friend's black eye and swollen lip that him own stomach cramp like it hot-gobbled all three large round-the-world pizzas he's cooking in oven.

But you know what? Oldcat always admire friend afterward. Drawing a line, even a stupid Phantom Vanilla Cowboy Hat Line, well, that a hard task for any pizza boy to do. Who know, maybe even Papa Luigi, maybe even Pretzel of the United States sometime have trouble with same too.

Why, you may ask, is line-drawing so hard? That the real question. It seem simple enough—get pencil, ruler, and do. But then extra bumps and roundabout circles always insert sad selves: soon, like fractals gerrymandering a map, they necessary details. And then too, why that pink, pig-nosed eraser always having to wear itself to a stained black and grunting nub so quick by erasing one line after another? Lines important, they not old corncobs to chew.

We just not taught right, that it? Then why grade school not simply assign sterilized, stabproof protractors and teach line-drawing in geometry, grade two? Or even better, why pupils not learn to draw their own freehand lines in art appreciation?

People, they always complain about uselessness of art, which not like football or other practical broke-back sports. But reconsider: Line-drawing I & II would make for-sure, real-life, hands-on classes, would instruct our children so powerful that maybe even Alabama fans or

Strom Thurmond be willing to fund for an NEA grant.

But then, ha-ha, of course: those old hogs would need to buy a missile silo full of pink erasers and stabless protractors to re-draw their lines too.

Time Machine

Ms Puss, she twice month get hair done. Walk in, stare happylike at row of HUUUUUUUUUUUMMMMMMMMMMMMMMMM-MMMMMMM hair bonnets that implant secret brainwaves. Same talky woman always squirt, cut, rub, burn Ms Puss' hair and tell Ms Puss what juice she learn about Sallie, Jackie, Thomassette, and Anne. Anne have husband who guzzle beer like reverse fire hydrant, Thomasette lose second baby cause she smoke and drink, Jackie dating some secret married man, Sallie lose job at plant.

Ms Puss' brain curl just like hair at so much news being so much bad. Talky woman say, "Oh Ms Puss, this hair do make you look so young!"

Perched alone under time-machine hair bonnet going HUUUUUUUUUUUUUUMMMMMMMMMMMMMMMMMMMMM, Ms Puss slink-think timewaves to happy days of being child: in that dream machine, her watch dirty-mouth boys steal green apples, throw down to her, laugh, laugh, and laugh. One boy with applejuice gooing round mouth, he a lawyer now. Sigh. *Further* back, go further back, she warn self: you married woman now. HUUUUUUUUUUUUUUUU-MMMMMMMMMMMMMMMMMMMMMM. She then slink-think of silly fair where her dad and mom take her to petting pen to touch silly, smelly goat and scared rabbit pink-eyes. Hee-hee, she remember smelling goat on hand, then tasting cotton candy and riding ferris wheel later. EEEEE-wwwww. She remember dark journey in big haunted house with many skeleton glowing everywhere. Ooooohh, she remember hearing skinny barkers yap-a-lap while jangling coins in many aprons.

HUUUUUUUUUUUUUUUUMMMMMMMMMMMM. Hairdryer quit; Ms Puss awake. Stylist, she come untangle hair/brain.

Ms Puss stop, look, listen, think at crossroads: Clang! Clang! Freight train coming!

A secret married man. That damned Jackie Babe. I wonder: she squirting between bedsheets with my Oldcat? That mysterious married man who no one know who—he my Oldcat? Ms Puss ponder like Miss Marple to sort through many not so happy clues of phone calls gone dead, perfume on Oldcat's clothes, silence from once friend Jackie, and too, too much money left in Oldcat's pocket after too, too many night supposedly at Oysterhead Lounge. Ms Puss study women reading magazines in hair salon then pinch back of hand and wish she a neanderthal in a cold cave who'd never read a detective novel in life and who constantly carried large, spiked club in right hand. . . .

"—Your hair so pretty. All the girls wish they had your hair. Just the other day, Jackie was saying she ought to dye her hair so it looked like yours."

Shut up Talky Woman, just shut up. Put me back under time machine again, please if you do. All me want is to sneeze pollen, climb apple tree, watch out for dinosaur thump and never, ever grow up.

Especial Interest

Damn and double dog damn!

Oldcat know it always a miserable mistake to listen to TV. Tonight no exception, for on news as Ms Puss away taking nursing class, he hear:

"If this was happening to white, middle class America, there would have been a cure for AIDS within nine months."

Oldcat scream, throw dirty shoe at TV, knock remote click-click off onto dog on floor. Why this young he-she on television screen so righteous? My father, a white, middle-class American, he die at 58 years of age from a heart attack. My mother, a white, middle-class American, she die at 64 of uterine cancer. When I was child, my neighbor, she die of bulbar polio. She nine years old, and guess what? She was a white, middle-class American.

Let us delimitate and see: yes, indeed, there a cure for polio now, after thirty year. But what about cancer and heart disease? All them white, middle-class Americans still dying from same; and polio, it even make comeback in democratic public school system where standards lowered until slugs like my neighbor's kid Jim Calley can make honor roll and be paraded red, white and blue on his dad's bumper sticker. Much more democracy, we soon have to cross final color-sex barrier and serve gray, middle-class, unisex dumplings at Lion's Club.

Oldcat stare at righteous, indignant interviewee who meantime have worked self into screeching fit on TV. Where these he-she people coming from just not so clear. They maybe think every government money and scientist funnelled into white male prostrate research? Say what? They think medical laboratories nationwide researching how to grow penises eight inch long and cottony white, instead of six inch and dirty pink? Say what? These he-she people want to take away from sickle-cell-anemia research, for maybe example? Or how 'bout MS? Or breast cancer? Or diabetes? Nobody with politically correctum need to eat that damned much sugar anyway, right?

"Wake up!" Oldcat shout to resilient TV that just stare stupid-like back. He then pick up click-click and turn off still yapping, still shrill voice.

Oldcat walk to stare out back door onto meadow to count to one trillion. One, two, three . . . After all, AIDS not the only sad-making disease on North American continent, gays not the only special interest . . . four, five, six . . . they just the special interest that presently screech the loudest . . . seven, eight, nine . . . got a damned alley tom can do that . . . ten, eleven, twelve . . . that mean it deserve lobster thermidor and shrimp étouffé when whole rest of family munching fried river cat?

Days in the Sun

Every honeybee in Summons County buzzing, cause Ms Puss going to be bridesmaid for best friend Jackie Babe in luscious June wedding. Ms Puss, who awake early wedding morning after all-night Tuscaloosa bachelorette bash with Jackie and three other girlfriends, of sudden sit up, pat stomach, and think back to ten nights ago whooppee-time with Oldcat and know something growing right. She watch dawn arrive and have to bite lips not to tell Jackie Babe, who after all readying to have her special day in the Alabama sun. Ms Puss also been have to bite lips all last night, all last month, cause this groom, in her opinion, be better to change first letter of name and get swept away . . . B-room. . . .

Sure enough, both Ms Puss's feelings prove right: she is pregnant, and Jackie's day soon eclipse in near quickest time ever, for broom-groom get in fistfight on wedding day, stay drunk for three week or more, go "hunting" many an all night (though it clearly out-of-season), until tearful Jackie Babe finally make appearance at court house and end unfair affair in four months, two weeks, one day.

After hearing court judgment, Jackie and Ms Puss sitting on Faunsdale cattle farm where Ms Puss's uncle recently dig catfish pond, envisioning it as futurest new business in Alabama. Jackie Babe, she hop out of white convertible, kick off shoes and uncork her combination celebration-wake bottle of expensive champagne called Dom Perignon, of which Ms Puss—whose stomach now clearly showing result of her and Oldcat's nighttime tomfoolery—allow herself only one glass. Ms Puss's uncle sit down on grass bank and share one glass too, but he got to go work now, plant rye seed for winter and cattle, so he finish quickly, pat Jackie Babe on arm, and walk into sun like lost cowboy movie.

"I think he's cute," Jackie whisper.

Ms Puss roll her eyes.

"Really. I mean it. Why'd your aunt ever leave him anyway?"

"She told us it was because he was messing around, but I found out when I was seventeen that it was her instead. I caught her and this guy in the back of her antique shop, on a huge four-poster bed."

Jackie Babe laugh at that. "He have a son?" she ask.

"Jackie, you're hopeless. Let one divorce rest. Why don't you try going out with Tom again?"

Jackie just sigh. "We're too much alike."

"You and me, or you and Tom?"

"Me and Tom of course."

"If that's so, you'd be the first X and Y chromosomes to resemble one another."

Ms Puss no doubt say this cause she of recent had amniocentesis and thinking of biology. Jackie Babe shake her golden curls in the October sun and toss what look like rabbit pellets into pond, to see catfish fighting in frenzy to eat them.

"X's and Y's?" she ask.

"Male and female . . . fighting like those catfish," Ms Puss add.

"Do you suppose it's just the males in there, fighting the females?"

Ms Puss, she been feeling X and Y twins kicking one another all morning, so she tempted to answer yes. But summer still clinging to Fall air and she too optimistic for that fatalistic biology.

"No. It's just that . . ."

In truth, she really no know *what* it just that, for her hormones so messed with fraternal-sororal twins and Jackie's divorce that she lucky she not perched naked by pond on topsy-turved head, a Summons County yoga queen airing nether self to world-wide inspection.

"It's just that . . ." she repeat, but even a running start with the words get her no farther this time than last.

"I know what you mean. . . ." Jackie Babe add.

And for the moment, watching Ms Puss's uncle lankily mount a tractor in the distance, both of them bubbly happy to gather the sun's rays onto their skin and to believe that they do . . . know what they mean.

Thursdays

Good Old Days

Oldcat-child him ride train in good old days.

Click-clack, click-clack.

Across Kentucky countryside, him pee through bathroom peehole onto rails below.

Him ride in smoke-filled cars, hack hack.

Him see every mean face in every mean hillbill town glare angrily back.

Him debark toward town water fountain of marble, where whites may drink, him scuff shoe against cute belowable one of granite where "man's best friend" may drink. Then, at bent elbow, him spy stooped, rinkety rust fountain where "coloreds only" mustard drink.

Him so ashamed that he sit white hands on dirty brown park bench in gray-silver pigeon shit. Whereupon thence him hear Burma-shaved man under nearby dying black walnut tree hop-shout in eight-movement harmony about red communists planting yellow books in white schools, while flooding green fluoride into natural blue water. Young Oldcat stare: it just like skinny man conducting technicolor country music symphony.

"Oh no, we cain't! Oh no, we cain't! We cain't let, we cain't let!" surrounding Kentucky peoples bray at question man ask, thinking themselves maybe a Greek chorus in doomful tragedy. From nearby dirty dust brick, low-slung, second-story window, *I Love Lucy* bellow for girlfriend Ethel Mertz on TV.

Oldcat shake his tender eardrums, feel his still oozy hand, blink at blotted sun, realize his child legs can barely stand to make a stand.

But walk they do, for Auntie arrive at station and motion to him, swarm him with orchid-lavender or some-ever kind of dead-flower hug.

Him legs wobble even more, but they do carry him to car, whencefrom Auntie drive past town's first suburb, wherefrom sausage grease severely souse air since every same-same asbestos-siding home sport same-same kitchen interior consisting of: ONE atomic-age vinyl breakfast bar, ONE X-ray-green, electric-age can opener, ONE happy pre-drug-age mother on many tranquilizer and pep pill, to guard herself from being mean just like Auntie, and ONE—

"Ow!"

"What you day-dreaming about? Pay attention," Auntie say, after pinching Oldcat's ear.

Soon through the tiny model suburb, they reach Auntie's boarding home only to hear more TV, this time about pretty co-ed at Lexington hometown Transylvannia College being strangled with own bra.

"That's what happens in the place you live," Auntie say.

Oldcat still feel pigeon mush on hands and agree. On TV, somber newsman in white shirt and skinny tie finish with dead co-ed, then switch to stubbly Vice President Richard Nixon and bubbly Premier Nikita Khrushchev butting billygoat heads in Kitchen Debate.

"That's what happens when you let communists in. Time for your bed. Best place for child this late of night."

Late? It barely summer twilight.

Next morning, Oldcat wake to salty bacon and toasted white bread afloat on scummed pond of country butter. Him boyhood blood pressure already rollicking in premature tidal panic when it notice photo in newspaper where Khrushchev bangle size 13 shoe on UN table. Then Auntie tune to *Morning Farm News* on TV, fine adjust sound until a hill twang pierce the air like fighter MIGS strafing hungries in Hungary or maybe coloreds in Little Rock. Puddled just to the right of newspaper, two egg yolks stare at young boy Oldcat, their cholesterol eyes like those of an avenging angel barring Paradise. *What's the matter, boy, ya yellow?* they ask.

"Now's the time ta be spraying yer tobacc-y," skinny TV Kentuckian screech like he imitating Lucille Ball, who last night imitating an Appalachian hillbilly in show about being picked up for speeding by

Tennessee deputy who sure-suspect her Cuban husband to be some type of international spy.

"That's your third cousin Orville talking on TV," Auntie say.

We bury you, Khrushchev's jowls meantime lowly modulate from newspaper photograph.

Fat man, fat man, oh please to do, Oldcat answer, holding head as his tinny pitchfork blind the two stupid, runny eggs. *Please to do and quick, before some adult fool claim these be good old days.*

A Cappella, Solo

Oldcat, one college weekday night him drink with friend named Craig. So sad they drink, so happy. They silly enough that they harmonize "Hang Down Your Head Tom Dooley" at Gainesville bar tables for beer. Customers fear them coming like Jehovah's Witnesses—but instead of money, people donate warm beer and hope duo creep coolly away, leaving no dregs. Craig, him reddish hair curl and him big jokey teeth laugh with each free mug, each bent note. Oldcat, he follow more like puppy than self, cause when him follow, he forget about broked back and snipped football career. Sing, sing, the day will never bend.

Old moon (Do we call her old because she so hoary, so wise— or because she dead lump of rock?) smile her twisty smile toward round planet earth as Oldcat stumble-bumble home, still whistling "Hang doown yer head and cry. Po Bo' yer bound to die."

Wednesday draggle forward like hunchback's evil hump, and friend of friend lank toward Oldcat, who plopped in chair of Student Center lounge during lunch, slyly wish-watching pretty co-eds who strut into cafeteria, pretending to read French paperback in hand.

"Oldcat, you hear what happen? Craig's dead."

Oldcat look up and think: *Impossible. Me just sing with last night. Impossible that such strong talisman be overcome. This person make silly college boy joke.*

Oldcat respond: "Ha, ha."

Friend of friend look angry-lanky, long-eye direct into Oldcat's. "No man, I'm serious. He was killed in a car wreck on Tallahassee Road."

"But I was with him last night. How?"

"He was at a party and borrowed Dee-Dee's Mustang to get beer and drove it at sixty over a hill through a stop sign."

Oldcat rub elbows on cushioned chair, look at French book, and wonder how come *he* no invited to Dee-Dee's party.

Friend of friend shake head and leave, Oldcat still refuse to believe until more friends say, "Yes, it's true: Craig ran a stop sign and blasted a Mustang into a cattle truck on Tallahassee Road."

Same time, next day, friend of friend return, one tall leg plodding before other like responsibility itself: "Craig's funeral is tomorrow at ten. Are you going to go?"

Oldcat, oh yes, him make many stupid decision in his jigsaw puzzle life, and look out, here tumble one now: Because see, him feel so sorry for self after football injury; because see, him not get invited to party and Dee-Dee would certainly never let him drive fancy Mustang car; because see, him just fumble-reading in original French big existential book called *L'Etranger* and on consequent him chest hairs burn romantic as *La Rivière Seine's* black dew; because see . . . but then *because see* no really matter, for stupid decision made: Stranger Mersault no cry or even *chanter le blues* at Momma's funeral, so Oldcat no gonna cry at friend's. After all, good ol' existential Craig would no want Oldcat to attend stiff, formal, fuddy American funeral: him would want Oldcat to sing forever "Tom Dooley" song at Palmetto Club Bar.

A cappella, solo I sing, therefore guaranteeing that most individual I surely am. Duty, pah! Righteous, philosophical Oldcat jerk foot like he tripping over leap of faith, then look up at friend of friend to sniff, "No, me no believe in funerals."

Friend of friend scowl and never laugh like friend again. In fact, his lanktime legs so angry that they break seven university lounge tiles while stomping away.

You ask: How many of life's pages it gonna take before romantic Oldcat understand why?

More than big exit-stenchial book hold, whether it printed in high French or pig-English, that for sure.

Blossoms

Oldcat and Ms Puss, concretely after they married, travel to Mexico. There they buy chess boards, St. Francis statues, money clips, a guitar fiddled by hand, Dos Equis beer, but never, never do they drink the water.

On bridge from El Paso to Nuevo Juarez, little children who not sick enough to just lie and die, they bobble and beg: "Let me carry, let me carry!" They jump, shout and hustle, hoping to tote tiny packages that American tourists clutch in so-hungry consumer hands.

Only for smallest nanosecond in subatomic particle Einsteinian history do Oldcat and Ms Puss think these children cute, for open sores inhabit brown arms and legs like angry fireants scrambling over kicked Alabama sand mound.

Farther on into Nuevo Juarez streets, girls carrying flowers and who-know-what diseases smile craftily at Oldcat, display light brown legs, rumps, tits, lips, and slinky eyes. "Buy my flower, Mr?"

Ms Puss, she push in front to buy instead. "That a lot for a flower," Ms Puss comment, and Mexican girl only smile and wiggle bare toes—whose nails are painted same gaudy color as petals of rose.

"I think . . ." Ms Puss say, but she let the thought go and carry rose down street. But so many men glare at her as she sniff and twirl that she finally toss it away onto refrigerator carton left in gutter. "I know . . ." she say.

Oldcat hear shuffle inside of carton and jump, leading Ms Puss quickly on for fear of bubonic rat.

But while Ms Puss staring in storefront window of Tex-Mex Western wear half a block away, Oldcat look back to see a ten-eleven-year-old girl emerge from refrigerator carton home and retrieve the blood rose bloom that Ms Puss had tossed. He watch girl spit to wet fingers, then straighten her hair, open two buttons on her blouse, bite lips to make them swolled, wiggle toes, then shift hips toward two young American soldiers who stumbling her way. Better not to tell Ms Puss what her tossed rose blossom into, Oldcat wisely decide—even if she not really plant or even graft the shoot.

"Oldcat, these boots are so cheap. Let's buy a pair."

See, Oldcat tell self, *someone make an honest living in land. It possible.* But sudden vision of warped, brown-skinned boy bending in sunlight by some mud adobe, pulling arms back and forth to tool boot leather, his ribs and collar bone heaving with each tug, this vision toss itself into Oldcat's mind like poster of Our Lady of Guadelupe tossing roses onto kneeling peasants.

He look back to street, but neither girl, nor rose, nor soldiers there.

"Oldcat, are you listening? Look at these boots."

One hour later, he and Ms Puss stop in shop for beer since they thirsty. (No drink water! No drink water!) On shelf they spy bottles of vanilla extract: one quart cost seventy American cent. "Aha, they use this to make Kahlúa Coffee Liqueur," Oldcat say, clutching his new boots. Mexican behind bar smile gold-tooth smile and swat fly away.

"Shu kidding?" nearby young American soldier laugh, puckering down on lime. "That shtuff's 160 proof 'n' cheaper 'n wine. They drink it here." Soldier weave, the Mexican behind bar smile gold tooth smile and swat another fly.

Back out on street, Oldcat and Ms Puss pass a vendor pushing his cart of meat. Oldcat, while watching the meat bounce in open air to send flies swarming, creates a political riddle: How many hot chili peppers would it take to render the protein of swarming blowfly eggs spicy and sweet? Answer: *E Pluribus Unum.*

They walk on, and soon at a Thursday afternoon cathedral, Ms Puss stop to photograph. Spires loom silently above her camera lens, like her grandmother's knitting needles. Two brown women walk up steps, tug at door, then enter, the door's heavy wood and metal almost pushing them and trailing dust in. Oldcat think door maybe going to catch part of their tattered Fall-green shawls or crush their bony flank, and he grimace, remembering terrible strapping machine at Gainesville newspaper plant that he always fear going to take off a finger.

"Let's go in and see, let's go see," Ms Puss say.

But inside, Oldcat and Ms Puss get breath sucked up into ceiling like it a cavern, for many, many women veiled and hunched from life are kneeling in pews, praying to full-sized bleeding Christ over altar and blood-drenched saints, of suspicious brown hue along all the walls. Most women keep so still that they resemble huge bats perversely clinging to floor. Some women, though, march slowly along the walls, their eyes caressing the mangled Jesus scenes hung there.

"What in world they doing?" Oldcat ask.

"Those are called 'the stations of the cross,'" Ms Puss read from brochure in a whisper to Oldcat. "They're walking them like Jesus did."

One nearby woman wearing the dullest black cloth Oldcat ever seen, she kneel and hunch shoulders until they curve like the cathedral arches above. Oldcat shift leg, fearing him back maybe going to start its usual hurt. All in all, it so quiet under the skeletal arches that he think himself to hear a knitting needle clack, or was that a thorn piercing flesh?

Oldcat and Ms Puss stand and watch—how long?

How long do a minute mean to people rotating on rocket ship planet grinding through space, query jesting Einstein, holding up an atomic finger to lift his archaic Mexican sombrero.

No matter how long, it not short, yet no softly treading women depart, but only shuffle their black and their brown rags, to cling like stubborn winter leaves. And after all, Oldcat understand, what fruitful there be for them to go outside this cathedral and its gory Calvary tree? All these stoop-shouldered women much too pruned to paint toes and sell rose blossoms on street, even should they be lucky enough to find one discarded by naive American tourists.

Finally, Ms Puss sway, grab Oldcat and lead him forward. He hold back, but in pew stained with human oil and no doubt tears, she kneel and motion him, crinkling brow until he do also, whereupon he feel knees pop, though they not really Catholic or even chiropractic.

"Christ keep us," he hear Ms Puss pray, "from a country or time when so many sweet girls carry blossoms, yet so many women never bloom."

"Amen," he hear himelf answer. "Amen."

Thems

One morning at office after angry black male employee stomp out, Oldcat realize him have more black friends when he young than now, even though Summons County nearly seventy-percent filled with that darker brethren and sistren. Oh, it not like him ever been stupid and say, "Some my best friends . . . ," but him *did* have black friends, especially in sportball. And once him even date black girl named Ruthie. She/he combination so strange though, that they both decide while segregation not good national, it certainly best personal policy.

But changing attitude of now concern Oldcat. Black workers in Summons County Electronics plant glad-hand, then sulk like they step-and-fetch extras in some lousy forties' Hollywood movie. Yes, this a rural Alabama town, but great leveller TV surely bring this lowliest of poverty county closer to real world than that. Or maybe that the point: TV make them jealous, show them just what is real world?

Them, Oldcat think. I already pick up Summons County habit. Them. It the white code word encrypted to represent other side, like they giant unmentionable atomic ants that best thing to do with is shoot in antennae, leave to dry in hot desert sun. Them.

So . . . *does* TV show "them" just how unleveled things are now perching in America? Is that the problem? Oldcat consider the local county bastion of racism, Summons Academy, where white Jesus and righteousness just naturally mix, like vanilla icing and angel food cake. But hey, shoe size fit both foot, no? If "nigger" and football cheers all that taught at Summons Christian Academy, "cracker" and football cheers all that taught at Carpenterville Public High. It create a never-ending daisy-chain of "thems."

I only a little big man, Oldcat worry—not Ronnie Reagan or

Georgie Bush. But it not take a big man to see that something glunk wrong in USA. When, oh when, a big man come to lead us from ignorance and break this sad them daisy-chain?

—Agh Oldcat! Caught you worrying again, didn't I? Good thing there no psychiatrist residential in Summons County, or all this subterranean worry place you on Valium and hand restraints.

Sure, okay, I worry, but what about rest of country? Oldcat respond to second self, meanwhile fingering his savings passbook in case he need to expatriate to Cuba or some other safe country to avoid race war. *There even more "thems" out there in urbana, so what about rest of country? After all, not every city-dweller able to afford psychiatrist or even big bar tab. Some lucky just to buy Doberman or Uzi on five-year extended payment plan.*

—That so true, second self reply. *That so true. . . . So maybe a mail order psychiatric shop offering cut-rate restraints, anti-depressants, self-help books, do-it-yourself Rorschach blots, and MMPI tests through UPS might turn a smart investment for a bright fellow like you.*

Oldcat pat his cobalt-blue savings book near his heart and rethink jumbo jet expatriation to Caribbean, cause after all and really, Alabama plenty too hot enough and him afraid legless of hurricanes from college time when living in Florida.

Yes, a fine investment, he finally agree.

—You can print catalogue on the office computer, take to Tuscaloosa and Kinko-Print thirty thousand, Oldcat's second self burble. *Show picture of slender feminine wrist in bedside leather restraint, show bright blue and red pills lounging in bottle, show yogi masters standing on head to see angels, show syringes spewing semi-jism—even start magazine, call it* ***Psychology Tomorrow,*** *so that it present forever up-to-date self-help articles.* Second self feel so smug that it prompt Oldcat to reach for fat green imported cigar. *I tell you, the only amazing thing be that no corporate raider yet reveal his red-blooded patriotic concern and do all this. It up to you, Oldcat, to be inventive Rebel Yankee Doodle Dandy, be like Sam Walton and dog Ol' Roy, show Southern initiative, beat them to it.*

Them. Oldcat stare at some slipping movement in room, sliding with heat of mid-morning sun. Dust? Brain cells? Leftover nigger-redneck nerve gas after argument with black employee? Just how many thems exist to boggle America?

Ah no . . . Oldcat perceive that the slipping movement is coming from fat-cat smoke of his own greenly imported Jamaican cigar.

However many thems exist to be, he tell self after giving puff and nose-sniff, *you're finely stinking just like one of them.*

Sign of the Times

I.

Oldcat just been promoted to vice-president not six month ago when a he-cannot-believe-it happen. Black supervisor named Andrew rush past secretary into office to shout that some guy is standing in back parking lot with rifle, shooting full beer cans off top of another guy's head.

Oldcat drop last Hostess Twinkie bite into rumen and leap from desk toward door. "Call the police," he tell secretary on leaving office, still tasting whipped cream from his chin. Him stop, glance around for baseball bat or cattle prod, but no chance—new Japanese-designed offices been constructed for civilization, not Alabama, so he run on.

"Evidently, the two guys are placing bets with everyone," Andrew tells Oldcat as they trot down the newly polished hall that glow creamy white, reminiscent of inside artery of Twinkie.

"Where're these idiots from?" Oldcat ask.

"They work here. Just started. In shipping and receiving, I think."

"Great."

Whang! . . . . Whop!

This what Oldcat hear from warehouse. He also hear low whistling and cheering from workers outside. Once he near loading dock he spot skinny white man with rifle in arm nodding to workers in parking lot while another skinny white fifty yards away pick up two beer cans from a case near his foot. This second white, he covered with foam from previous burst beer cans and look somewhat like Monster from Black Glugoon.

Springtime sunlight already raise hot and wavy air from the blacktop, and Oldcat pull back from heat on instinct since he sit in air-conditioning all morning.

"Get three uv'm this time!" The first skinny one with the rifle shouts to the second skinny one with the foam. Then he turns to the workers: "One off top the other'n. I'll shoot 'em each one off'n his head there. Place your bets in the—"

"No more bets!" Oldcat shout. "And no more shooting! You two need to put up that rifle and those beer cans and come to my office."

The idiot with the .22 turn to Oldcat, lazy-pointing the rifle more toward the foot of the loading dock than any personal-effects part of Oldcat. Still . . . Oldcat glad to see Tom stalking behind the idiot standing so skinny with the rifle.

"We ain't doin' no harm out here," that one shout back in a shrill hill twang. "Hit's a free country, ain't hit? There ain't nothin' can git shot in that empty field back there."

"Nothing but your friend. Put the rifle up and come inside to talk to me—both of you."

"Well just what're you gonna do if we don't? Who're you anyway?"

Oldcat see the rifle beginning to rise toward him. He also see Tom take the man in low bear hug and slam him into nearby parked green car—*That James Johnson's emerald antique Mustang?* Oldcat stupidly wonder before he jump from dock and run toward fight. Several men are grabbing for the money that's spilled from the knocked-over coffee tin, and the second capital I idiot who balanced beer cans on his head is running for the fallen rifle. Oldcat block-tackles him, just like good old college days at U of F, throwing him into a climbing rose bush, then punching him three hard times in the sternum until Skinnyneck double over and gasp for mother's air. Oldcat pull leg back to kick him in nose, but the already sour smell of beer repulse him, so he stop. Also, he remember that he a vice-president now and must show decorum, as Japanese so fond of telling administrators. *Noblesse Oblige is what they mean,* Tom always say. And when Oldcat always answer, *Huh?,* Tom just shake his head to tell him he should read more.

Oldcat now look back to Tom, who only a supervisor and so can freely slam Idiot #1 one more time like he a cowboy dummy in a rodeo. Man flop stupidlike, so fight over, even though no official blow whistle or toss in towel. *Ah,* Oldcat think: *maybe that what Tom mean by noblest of leaves.*

Excitement over now too, so more employees begin bending for bills that floating in soft breeze.

"I want all that loose money returned to whoever bet it! And whatever loose money from that tin belonged to these two, I want them to get it back. Ricky, Juan, Andrew —" Oldcat pick three responsible men, mixing his races politically as he always make a point to do—"I want the three of you to see to it, all right?"

They nod at Oldcat just as two police cars bounce into the lot. Oldcat hear moan from ground behind and turn with clenched fist, but second skinny man hold up his arm and cower: "I hain't gonna do nothin', Mister. I'm just standing up, that's all, honest."

Two hours later, after police drive idiots to jail for discharging a weapon inside city limits, disturbing the peace, resisting arrest, drunken and disorderly conduct, and probably peeing in public and animal abuse thrown in too, Oldcat stand once again in creamy Hostess Twinkie corridor, drinking Diet Coke with Tom. Since him adrenaline just about worn down, Oldcat notice that his back hurting from the tackle—funny thing, though: it not hurting in old football injury place, but high above. He roll shoulder, feel a pop, then pain go away.

"Back hurting?" Tom ask.

"No, it never felt better. Exercise good for it, better than a chiropractor."

"Ha. That's great," Tom say. "Maybe we should hire some more idiots and arrange tackling practice for you every day."

II.

At supper, Oldcat tell Ms Puss what happen. She worry until she sure he all right, then she, who been taken with town priest and learning about Catholicism so to judge if they should send their twins to interracial parochial school that who knows how wound up in hard-core Baptist Summons County; then she laugh and say: "You know what today is, Oldcat? The Feast of the Annunciation of the Blessed Virgin Mary. Better known as The Visitation."

"So?"

"So, that's when the angel came to tell Mary she was pregnant with Jesus. Maybe those two visiting your lot today were devils, not angels, visiting to tell you something."

Ms Puss been so upset about children's education that she even talking about relocating to big city lately. Oldcat take this into account, roll eyes at her nonsense, then look for newspaper.

Between Oldcat's bites of blackened catfish for supper, the phone ring and he pick it up to hear Two-Way, Carpenterville's crazed assistant police chief: "Just thought I'd call and tell you, Oldcat, that the skinny one who did the fancy rifle shooting vowed he was gonna kill you and Tom. Course he's still half drunk, but I just thought I'd tell you. We're gonna leave them both in jail for ten days then follow them and their piece-a-shit car to the county line. Their rifle'll get lost in a creek somewhere, but just thought I'd tell you."

"Thanks," Oldcat say.

. . . Late that night when the moon strike strange and blue, two catfish flip upwards in Oldcat's stomach, twitching their whiskers and munching cottage cheese and honey. "Forget noblest of leaves and decorum," they both advise Oldcat with a nasty slurp and flick of whiskers. "You live in America, ah so, no? Buy a cattle prod, some electric fence, maybe two-three rottweilers and a 12 gauge pump shotgun. Teach your children reading, writing, arithmetic, and karate in the safety of your home, and always keep a chiropractor on company retainer."

Oldcat toss, trying to wake and smartly question the catfish, ask them maybe if there really is an X-ian god or at least something spiritual and floaty in the world like the Roman Catholic and other religions say, but the fish vanish toward Ms Puss's feet to submerge in blankety murk, leaving not even the empty dog bowl they'd swilled cottage cheese from.

What a vision!

Him hear street lamp buzz outside and reach for Ms Puss's shoulder, wondering if he should wake her, but then he stop. The Visitation. Sure, this just how Mary felt when angel came. No doubt she not wake Joseph to say, "Guess what? Baby not yours, but belong to God."

He stare out window, trying to spot moon. Maybe it give spiritual answer, if catfish won't. But no moon appear, and he wake up enough to realize that the catfish visitation was really just a dream. The silence, though, that real enough, and that same silence a real enough sign of the times, too. Just watch ignorance in action and keep mouth shut—that your only job as American citizen. Put pillow over your head and . . . and Oldcat then sleep-toss in terrible dream of rottweilers, catfish, shotguns, hillbillies, niggers and rednecks.

But in the morning, he go downstairs and take toast from Ms Puss, tell her to sit at breakfast bar."You have got to hear this: I'm gonna tell you a dream I had about catfish," he say, giving the toast a good scritch with butter knife. . . .

"What it mean?" she ask when he finished.

"It mean that I agree with you: we going to enroll kids in Roman Catholic integrated middle school. It mean that silence no longer work, I'm tired of being quiet."

Even as Ms Puss hug him, Oldcat envision .22 floating to surface of nearby dirty Sucarnochee River, see local yokels Tim Moore and Bill Turner who perennially run for sheriff on hang 'em high ticket, grabbing rifle and shouting, "Let's go shoot that nigger-loving Florida Yankee!"

That yet another visitation, though, yet another sign; better to save it for yet another time.

Cold Sores, Body Odors, and Credit Cards

Oldcat and Ms Puss visiting her parents who just sold cattle and catfish farm to uncle and retired in Florida when Ms Puss happenstance to tell her mother that they in credit card crunch big time cause of buying x, y, and z—not to mention kindergarten clothes for Meow and Grrr. Father overhear and say him help out, write check for how many moneys—three, four, five hundred, what it take to pay off a credit card anyhow?

Ms Puss turn plastic white, like someone's overdrawn bank statement. "We have six cards, Dad. We owe over a thousand dollars on each one."

Dad-in-law yell so hard and loud that Oldcat come run from bathroom, pulling up trousers, thinking burglar who been lurking Florida neighborhood gnawing his way through front door and threatening poodle, family, and children all three.

"*SIX? SIX* credit cards? How can anybody with the least bit of maturity fall for something as stupid as that? What are the two of you doing? What are you thinking? You're obviously *not* thinking! What are you teaching my grandchildren?"

Oldcat swallow both stomach and fist he making, seeing Ms Puss shaking and ready to cry since father screaming so loud.

"Geees!" Father explode.

Oldcat know that father-in-law always say this whatever-it-mean word when he being disgusted by lifeform lower than high Episcopalian.

"Geees! I was willing to help you two with a reasonable amount, but I'm not a bank, you know. I owe money too—at least I save my credit expenditures for major purchases, though. Why can't you two . . ."

Yak-a-rack-a, yap, yap! Father-in-law's mouth working like greasedy oil derrick on side of country road, but spewing all those irrelevant sermony American Gothic words instead of valuable oil, until Oldcat wish he just revert to *Geees!* After all, this no way to spend X-mas vacation.

Mom-in-law try her usual intervention tactic: "Does anyone want a piece of pie? I just made it this . . ." But pie no work this time.

Yak-a-rack-a, yap, yap! Father-in-law riding on doozy of derrick so high it spew like offshore oil spill.

And once more Ms Puss get headache and once more Oldcat promise himself he not travel to this subtropics Florida home for two year or more—maybe not even until first woman get elected President, cause that surely kill dad-in-law.

That night they watch TV—sometimes easier than talking to one another, yes? One eternal youth come on in a commercial to announce all gosh and folksylike, "We have a secret, right? I mean we both get these ugly droozling cold sores. But I cured my mine with Blistex and you can too. Doctor Approved." Then a woman come on, whisper all pouty-seductiony-like, "Morning breath like city dump on Arbor Day? No gettum good-bye kiss, but typewritten refrigerator note instead? Then try Listerine: it helps fight ugly morning breath blues." TV on a roll: it telecast entire panacea parade for swollen anuses, itchy jocks, soggy nostrils, and body odors—never once time, though, do it dare offer cure for credit cards.

Of course not, Oldcat think, looking at grumped dad-in-law slouching in armchair: *some things just too sacred for even the magic screen.*

Ye Junque Shoppe of Lyfe

Vice-president Oldcat hire horsey woman at plant. This not mean she rich blueblood from Kentucky with snout in air: it mean that when she talk her teeth show and she snort. Still, she perfect for job, because she trained safety officer who have to inspect each department, deal with many supervisors.

Oldcat hear her snort and haw-haw two, three department away sometimes, and him just smile.

Soon, rumor horseback around that safety officer a lesbian.

"That good," Oldcat tell one indignant supervisor. "That mean you no try to sexually harass her or she barbell your jewels."

But longer horsey woman work at plant, more she bittermoan like shin-splinted mare about "good old boy conspiracy." Oldcat hear this phrase galloping down halls, hear horsey woman cackling with other women, hear, "This supervisor stupid, him no able to do job—hired just cause he got a thing 'tween his legs . . . that supervisor stupid, him no able to do job—hired just cause he got a thing 'tween . . ."

Enough become enough. Oldcat bring horsey woman in for what he think going to be a reasonable talk.

Scream, yell, and slobber form around bit in her mouth like she accidentally set loose in hot field and eat jimson weed. Face turn red—apoplexy soon? Oldcat envision company paper headline looming: *Safety Officer Falls Coronary Victim in VP's Office!*

Oldcat finally have enough. They shoot horses when they lame, dogs when they mad—and this woman excesses both. "You fired. Pick up two week's pay tomorrow. Leave today."

Two days later when horsey woman cash check and file sexual harassment claim that she never going to collect under ten different blue Alabama moons, Oldcat tempted to draw grand moral like "No wonder they no want fags in Army!" But he hear him own self braying and see him own horsey teeth glinting the moment he think that. *OK. No moral,* he privately inform the green gargoyle patiently paperweighting his desk. *Gay or straight, she just like you: one more ugly-faced, mean-hearted bric-a-brac congregating in Ye Junque Shoppe of Lyfe. There plenty enough of fractured emerald to go around, if anyone care to form collection.*

The Last X-ian Burial

Oldcat, when him dad die, he haunt obituary columns for five-six-seven week, afraid that epidemic arrive. Who else going? Who else? Tiny black and white newsprint creep onward like skeleton fingertips and eye sockets. But nobody him know quit roosting, so he eventually forget.

And when him mamma die, same thing happen. Names sneaking

familiar this time though, and Oldcat fret that newspaper make mistake, reprint deaths from six and one half year before. Him stop reading obituary column after only five days—too much empty-marrowed bone-clack ascending from that graveyard print.

Time, it wonder-drugged him on. Parentless Oldcat kiss Miss Puss and children, go to work, thunder at stupid TV newscasts, play Trivial Pursuit, eat hamburger and onion for belly, drink Old Forester and water for cranium.

Then one night while browsing a newspaper in bathroom, him see where British Royal Prince Do-You-So-Call-Me, who carry high-toned proven sure-enough DNA from Queen Victoria and Russian Romanovs both, that same prince donate speck of test-tube blood, which big-brain scientists with math formulas like turnips bulging under brows will use to identify nine skeletons recently unearthed in the no longer USSR. It seem that the same old Lenin who exile Trotsky to dribble tequila in Mexico also ordered goodnik dumblies to shoot Czar Nicholas II, pretty wife Alexandra, and all of seven-child brood. So now, turnip-browed scientists wondering: these undugged calciums, they those same be-Czar skeletons?

When Oldcat read this, he squatting on Everyman's cold thinking throne, so it easy to imagine gleaming goodnik cohort crusading their communist bullets to gnaw into child bones; royal bodies then consequent falling like limped sausage; greasy-handed peasants then tossing black dirt over all nine lumps of drying DNA and death-white flesh. What cold season this happen in do not matter, for everyone know that Russia own nothing but hard times and snow.

Did some graceless angel flap wings like apocalyptic vulture over this last X-ian burial in USSR? Look! Watch! Little girl's torn ring finger twitch when peasant's heavy, comradely boot drive spade into her royal neck. Good-bye Romanovs. Sleep tight.

Oldcat flip through newspaper, watching quiet snowflakes fall on other side of shower curtain. Friend Tom loan him plenty British thrillers, so him know that many an exiled Russian Romanov prince or princess dringle semi-incognito through Europe this entire century. But they all just fakely prancing, if this test result positive. For if Romanovs all deaded long ago, then none living would have carried Prince Do-You-So-Call-Me's DNA in their skinnies. Instead, all that royal molecular mystery been buried static under Chernobyl snow for seventy some year.

Oldcat ponder: him daddy, he born in 1918. When Romanov czar dropping into snow, did daddy sametime feel thwack of doctory hand in Cincinnati hospital?

Oldcat look up, full of question now that him bowel empty. Could my DNA been ESP'ed from Russia? And if snowflakes really fall in my shower stall, when they evaporate, where they go? And why, oh why it so quiet on Alabama winter night? . . . Ah good. . . some neighbor have stupid dog that howl. Oldcat flip through newspaper to obituary column. So many bodies him no recognize. Him imagine them dumped at county landfill, with empty cold cream jar for pillow, moldy Cool Whip tub for bonnet, and a drunken government union employee sifting for—workers unite! Stop this mass death! Check all outgoing DNA! Bodies be not tubers, they too important to under dirt decay!

"—Oldcat! Oldcat, what you do in bathroom? You sick? You been in so long we worry."

"Okay. I okay, Ms Puss." But Oldcat, he look at dry shower curtain and wonder: death have such icy fingers for Romanovs, for Mamma and for Dad, what it save for me?

He listen to winter no-sound sound, then quickly pray, *Howl, dog, howl!*

A New Anthem

Oldcat, him take vacation trip with family to Florida. Him drive around ugly city of Jacksonville, think, Ha, glad me going to good ol' St Augustine where me and Ms Puss 1st met.

In back seat, twins Meow and Grrr sing "Star Spangled Banner" in key of pheew. Oldcat glance to Ms Puss, say that he never learn all of words. Ms Puss, she laugh and ask what "spangled" mean anyoldway.

Passer-by gang member, fourteen yearums young, he no laugh. Him face important initiation task. Him want to lose peach-fuzz, be big man. So from pickup he toss concrete block onto Oldcat family car. Physics rule hereonout ever. Block thunk, car go seventy swerve. Ms Puss thunk, lose brain blood and die. Child Meow thrown from car, scrape off many skins and lives, lose blood and fluid then die. Child Grrr bounce-bounce, break one bone, live. Oldcat lose left eye, break right wrist, and live.

Gang member, he too young, get five Ridalin pill and slapped hand, then go to tiny folk jail. Judge and jury clap palms, slap knees, and sing, "Have to wait, have to wait, have to wait to become a man" in syncopation to latest Ice-T top of chart hit.

Surprise! In tiny folk jail, gang member take steroids, grow beard and learn words to "Star Spangled Banner."—All dirty though, since they from MTV. Meanwhile, him eating sausage and pepperoni pizza and working out in tiny folk jail's gym, so he next time be able to throw two concrete block at once, one in each under-aged, fatherless hand.

Waaang, waaang!

This dream I have? Oldcat ask, sitting up in bed with heart pounding. Ms Puss alive next to me, my car safe in garage, we not even start vacation yet, not even got TripTik from Triple-A. Should I take two aspirin, warm water, and pray? Agh no, it just typical American nightmare. Back to sleep like rest of neighborhood: it sure to go away.

Fridays

A Backwoods Mare's Tale

Oldcat decide to grow Alabama beard after working seven months at Summons Electronics. It fur out so lush, so dark, so murky that him feel like Samson awaiting Delilah. Still, he jealous since friend Tom's beard more mature: it mix salt with pepper. And Tom say that black friend Andrew jealous of them both cause when he try to grow one it scratch like cold Brillo pad on hot iron skillet.

What the cause of this hirsute pursuit? Did Oldcat's brain cells niggle, *Beard make the man, just like clothes?* No, brain cells have no voice whatsoever in activities, cause his hormones in full stallion gallop. *We'll corral you a hunky filly, you just wait, pardner,* they and the beard tell him, enunciating no doubt through follicles, like a paramecium's cilia gone permanently wild.

With such a berserk beard, Oldcat trot to Friday night bar called The Brass Chimpanzee and meet Tom. About eight o'clock, a JC student slumlord named Ed ride a white mare through side door, knocking off his dirty white cowboy hat while doing so. Yeah, this scene playing about right for Summons County, Oldcat think as the mare's hip nudges a pool table, as everyone in Chimpanzee gawk and clap and bounce their beer bottles on bar, all which make the mare snort nervous flecks of slobber over customers and pool table felt.

Oldcat look to Joe, who own The Brass Chimpanzee. Joe not happy at all over Ed's joke nor the slobber speckling expensive green felt; in fact, Joe burn apoplexic red beyond normally fire engine face and hair, so Oldcat quick-review his recent-learned CPR, realizing there always be another, stinky side to any mare's tale, no matter how groomed and curried it be. Of sudden, mare bellow, more like gutshot wild sow than any Tennessee Walker—which of anyway it certainly not, if to judge from way planking clops so hollow. No, mare more like a Summons County Wobbler.

Bump, bump, snort, slobber—soon it clear that mare have to be shooed out back door, since no one—especially drunken Ed who's concerned only with finding his lost cowboy hat and not falling off the mare—can turn her around.

Now Oldcat, he worked on horse farm in high school Kentucky, so him have great faith in dog-food stupidity of horse flesh, also great respect for heavily heaving horse hooves, so he keep toes and body organs well out of range as mare clop past. Most other bar patrons feel the same, though one drunk junior college girl grab mare's tail and shout "Ride 'em cowboy!" and on consequent get one of Joe's barstools splintered by kicking hoof.

"Get the hell out of here!" Joe shout, for seventeenth time. "Someday someone's gonna crack your head for ya!"

Bleachy blonde girl motivate wide-eyed tear to swell as she stare scare-like at splintered stool and hear back door frame crack from mare's departing hips.

Minutes later, she still apologizing to Joe.

"That's okay, hon; I didn't mean you. It's all that damned Ed's fault for bringing a horse in here in the first place," Joe placate girl in his special voice that sound like dark chocolate being warmed on a winter-cough day.

He mainly say this, Oldcat know, since he always on moveout for young thing from local JC, claiming they all majoring in Life 101 and that somebody got to accept responsibility to teach them, cause cloud-clinging professors in ivory tower sure not.

After while, Joe get busy with customers, so this pretty young thing attach self with sweaty lips, tawdry tan face, and pencil hips to Oldcat and his Samson shag beard.

"She on drugs or something," Oldcat tell Tom in bathroom.

"Why d'you say that?" Before taking pee, Tom get big grin and stare at wall like meditating Buddhist monk.

"Cause she keep wanting to touch my beard, and cause her lips ut parents—their parents—not sleeping in wooden bed, but on floor.

"All your springs are sprung. That's stupid," Grrr comment brightly, ounding more like father-in-law every moment. Him even curl thick o-magnon brows just like Florida dad-in-law.

Oldcat, who been surprised at how much he been enjoying futon, arrow eyes at narrow-minded son and think: *Child-abuse squad would ick me up for going to garage and putting one of the discarded bed slats to e boy's head, but that seem only possible way to get through his thick enaged skull. Maybe we fed him too much cowmilk as infant.*

He continue to stare at angry son and plan a talk with Ms Puss about ating him between useless bed springs and bed slats then shipping him Tampa and dad-in-law, since they two existing so very much alike. here they can butt cro-magnon brows with one another and alligators d palmettos until one or both or all do crack. . . .

"Stupid," Grrr again comment, just in case deaf father not hear first ne.

"Not stupid," Oldcat counter after holding breath and considering tions, finally choosing the familiar in-law mode of argumentation over PS or child abuse. Nefertiti, she have these same child problems, or she t bury rapscallions in premature pyramid?

"Dad's right, you know, Grrr," Meow chimes in, walking up the ps to peek at the purple futon on the floor. "Futons are the in-thing— en in Alabama. Hey Dad, can I take the pick-up tonight? Some friends m school want to have a hayride."

This change of subject not shake Oldcat, for lately Meow been using r red-herring technique so well that both Oldcat and Ms Puss agree she ing to be either lawyer or politician, or both. This character shift came ut soon after she broke her arm on twelfth birthday and nearly died m blood poisoning.

"Who? Who's going?!" Grrr screams, taken aback. "Is Meilissa nton going? No one asked me!"

Maybe if I break just one of his legs, or ship just his head to Florida, leave ly under rose bushes out back, he'll improve and Child Abuse Squad will lerstand, Oldcat thinks while handing over jangling keys to Meow.

sweating so much they drip like the men's weight room at University of Florida, or like she that mare after racing for Triple Crown."

"Ha. Don't know why her lips are sweating, but she's probably grabbing your beard just cause she wants to wipe that mare's tail smell off from her palm." Tom shake his own peter, then give wash basin a sniff and decide his palm stay cleaner if he not wash in dirty Brass Chimpanzee sink. Wise, so wise a decision—this what meditation get you.

"Understand what I mean?" he ask, giving palm a sniff and making fake lunge for Oldcat's beard.

"Ha-ha. That's real funny."

But when Oldcat go back into main room, the young she is once more talking with Joe at bar, prancing her tan JC girl legs hard atop a footrest hurdle to jump Joe an apple-sweet kiss over a dill-pickle tip jar filled with pennies and quarters. Oldcat muse on what Tom said in bathroom as she miss kiss but neigh skittishly, kick legs, and try again. This time she connect with Joe, so Oldcat scratch beard. On pulling his hand away . . . sure enough, him smell horsey sweat from her palm, so friend Tom was right.

Oldcat hear pool balls clack, watch beer foam, hear JC co-ed whinny at Joe. He put beer can to forehead to cool it down, knowing damn well he should buy six pack and place cans much lower on anatomy. Girl kick and whinny again to give Joe one more kiss. But soon a crowd crawl in and Joe got to bartend full tilt—it too early for heavy flirting. So the tan girl work her way back to Oldcat after swaying her hips against three, five, eleven drunks who reach out, but no can touch.

Even as her perfume overcome mare's tail smell and even as Oldcat fall halfway in love, he hear Tom, who playing pool, snicker.

No wonder, Oldcat think, bunching his brows and squeezing neck of beer bottle, *no wonder Samson so very pissed at Delilah and the Philistines.*

Sure enough, there a Delilah and plenty of Philistines about, but seeing as there's no temple pillars around to pull down. . . .

"I'm majoring in secretarial science at the junior college," the tanned girl announce, nudging close so that Oldcat actually feel her pure, passionate perfume burn his sweaty forehead and delilate his nostrils.

"When I graduate, I'm going to move to At-lann-na and get me a real job."

She again grab Oldcat's beard; he start to pull away, then decide, *No, hell, let her.* What harm after all? Beard already stink, and it not require the gypsy palm reader living in brick house out on Highway 8 to foresee that this filly going to someday yank the wrong stud horse's tail and get rib-kicked bad, long before she ever leave for Atlanta, her Golden Dream City of the South.

A drunk leer by and girl swish her bottom like she shooing off a fly. *No, no trouble in foreseeing future at all, for she own a typical enough mare's tale for Summons County.*

Oldcat sigh and tug his beard where tanned girl just once more put her palm. And this Oldcat stallion standing here, he think, what about him? He got some dreary, backwoods Summon's county mare's tale awaiting him too, only difference being the sex is changed? Just what would the gypsy woman on Highway 8 foretell about him?

Soon, soon, sonny boy, my crystal ball foresee that if you keep eating your Wheaties those whiskers of yours will grow long, and form a fine stallion's mane. Oldcat blink, smell gypsy's perfume—rank and deep like possum gland—then he lean across green table to look into milky crystal ball, but she cover it with a moldy bar rag someone of previous have thrown up on. *That'll be forty-five dollar, sir, for telling your future and mare's both.*

He hear Tom laugh implike, and then he hear worn pool balls crack and scatter on the felt, some dropping in, some just trailing off in a mare's tale spin. . . .

Spring, not sprung

Passing of winter send change-bugs through Ms Puss, so she decide they going to buy futon and sleep on floor.

"Foo-ton?" Oldcat try Japanese word in mouth; it barely fit, but he know better, at this stage in life, to bother arguing with lovely Ms. Puss or Japanese either one—both nearly always have better ideas.

That night, as the twins finally return from their hayride—Grrr won his way and went along, which was dandy cause the house stayed four hours without MTV—that night, Oldcat is lying upstairs in bedroom on futon, listening to Ms Puss breathing and light rain falling outside, to his brain cells growing and dying inside. Then the word "stupid" drifts upward from kitchen, where Grrr no doubt is making a bologna sandwich. The word screams through Oldcat's mind like the marauding vapor of a cut onion.

Stupid.

A person, Oldcat decides, if he's cynical enough, if his brain and body cells are twisted enough, could use that single word to destroy not only futons, but Seven Wonders of World and all of life. Oldcat slides his arm across the restful, cool wooden floor and imagines a hieroglyphic mantra: *Futon stupid, Pyramids stupid, Marriage stupid, Love stupid, Courage stupid, Education stupid, Mall stupid, Sacrifice stupid, Family stupid, Religion stupid.*

Yes, someone with brain and/or cells garlicked enough could steal away all our capitol letters. Who was that famous poet who sign his name in only small letters? We study him in high school with sweet-smelling Miss Grey. No matter, cause him and Miss Grey both stupid too, cynical person would say.

As the rain continues to patter, Oldcat feels Ms Puss turn, hears her laugh in her sleep. Then he hear both dogs trumble through downstairs pet door. Him think maybe he can even smell mulch mulching and hear daffodil bulbs in yard pushing aside dead winter grass and musty dirt.

Yes, that dandy and fine: Hurray! Spring day coming soon. Go to sleep, Oldcat, he tell self, for Capitol Letter or lower case, not no one, Nefertiti or lowly onion-eating slave, *ever* say Spring stupid. Spring, that one thing that never be sprung.

Turtle Love

When Oldcat and Ms Puss first meet—on vacations in Florida of all places—Ms Puss been travelling from next county and going to JC—not knowing what in the world for, it just thing to do in Summons County area, like mountain climbers near Neverest, she guess.

In one math class she meet strange girl who for all of Ms Puss's two eyes appear to smile with baby teeth that still home-fed on Gerber's. Can this possibly be? Can an adult have never lost her baby teeth? Ms Puss so intrigued she talk with girl, find out that her name Sarah and that she and her husband are majoring in planning.

"What that?" Ms Puss ask, still staring at tiny teeth.

Ms Puss and Oldcat only been met six weeks now, so she come back from that Florida vacation full of heartthrob and unsurety, ready to question any any and every every.

"City and urban planning. Like streets and traffic lights and things. My husband is majoring in it, so I am too. He served on a submarine in the navy."

Girl have eyes so glazed that they look like hen's who's hatching eggs, Ms Puss think. *Ahh, with hen eyes and baby teeth like yours, lucky they no allow women on submarines or you major in scuba diving too, I bet. By the way, are those teeth in your empty head really your original baby teeth?*

But of course Ms Puss can no ask this—at least not yet.

"Does your husband go to school here?"

Girl smile and nod.

Of course, Ms Puss realize. Maybe those glassy eyes *are* laying a secret egg. Is she pregnant? Ms Puss wonder. Could the baby be stealing all her calcium and making her teeth small?

Three, five more time Ms Puss talk to her, find out that she and submarine husband met in Meridian, Mississippi, just as husband was leaving navy.

"I met my boyfriend in St Augustine," Ms Puss reply. "We were both on vacation. Can you believe it?" This the first time Ms Puss call Oldcat her boyfriend—she just want to try word in mouth, see how it fit. Much better than girl's baby teeth, she decide, still lacking nerve to ask about those phenom.

Seventh, ninth time they meet in class, girl invite Ms Puss to a party at her and submarine husband's student apartment.

"Submariner?" Oldcat reply, when Ms Puss tell him. "They all crazy, so we need to hide knives and guns in pockets and purse."

"Don't think so," Ms Puss say, picturing girl's baby teeth. And besides, she already meet husband once. He wear country cowlick like in old Elvis Presley poster and gap-tooth smile that barely let his soft, soft voice sneak through crevasse into public. "I just don't think so. Maybe we should take my Rook deck with us, though."

"Submariner? Rook?"

But Ms Puss right. This "party" the smallest definition she ever encounter of same: only one half of other invited couple show up, a male whose features so bland he resemble paneling in insurance office. So counting the pet turtle—which Oldcat, Ms Puss, baby-tooth girl and submariner husband, plus panelling person busily gaze at for first hour—they total six for party. Maybe panelling person wind up asking turtle out for date, if things go well.

Moresomeover than party being small, turtle couple serving only sweetened iced tea. They not even put out lemon on counter, not to mention student beer or whiskey. After second iced tea, even turtle appear cold and lonely, though outside broil a Deep South, May evening.

"We have a pet lizard too," the girl say. "He livths in the back closet and keeps roaches away."

Ms Puss for first time notice that girl has a tiny lisp. Also, she notice for the first time that Oldcat not listening to the girl's lisp or looking at her baby teeth, but watching her breasts, which project rock-hard and definitely not baby or tiny.

So Ms Puss grab Oldcat's arm and rub as they talk about turtle, lizard—and what else to enliven the party. Later, she mostly remember all-night sound of fork cutting plateful of canned green beans, white bread and bland meat loaf. After splitting last green bean and spreading it over plate in curious pattern that resemble Pennsylvania hex sign, panel-faced guest make his apologies and leave early. It been too much for even him. *Please don't take turtle out with you,* Ms Puss nearly cry as she watch turtle in bowl perform sudden flipper movement—it see golden chance and trying to escape party too? This evening certainly worse than being trapped on *Gilligan's Island* for eternity, so Ms Puss can not blame reptile, if so.

During dessert, Ms Puss decide that they really are baby teeth as she watch girl masticate last of strawberry shortcake. Her submariner husband watch too, so much in love that he dock in her bay forever, heedless of the world's permanent typhoons and hurricanes churning deeper waters outside port.

"How long have you two been married?" Ms Puss ask.

Turtle couple look at one another and smile, grab hands.

"Four years and four months," both say.

"Almost five," submarine husband add.

Five? Ms Puss think boy make elementary mistake in rounding number of years, but then she realize: *Ahh, five months. He counting carefully, going for Guinness Book of World Records.* She imagine the couple, surrounded by plastic green and yellow turtle islands, living in some future city they will design with green turtle bus stops and lizard-closet phone booths lining every avenue, bright yellow plastic sidewalks and ornamental green bean vines delineating streets, which all one-way, of course. She envision them tightly holding hands and walking down those same yellow sidewalks, urban masterminds unknown to everyone but two, maybe three city bureaucrats. Imagining this scene, she surprised to find herself so jealous she have to go to bathroom.

"Oldcat and I known one another for only a bit over one month . . . six weeks now," Ms Puss tell mirror in bathroom. *Rounded off, that nearly a year,* mirror answer. Ms Puss put on lipstick, smile, and walk out.

Submariner husband showing Oldcat photo albums. "Here's when Sarah was climbing the singing tower in Ocala. Here's when Sarah was lying on the beach at Gulf Shores. We got attacked by sand fleas right after. Here's when Sarah was outside Atlanta Hirschfield Airport. They employ sixteen city planners just for that airport. Here's when Sarah first bought our turtle at a mall in Montgomery. . . .

". . . and here's when Sarah . . ."

Ms Puss see Oldcat's head reel, so she scrounge in purse for Rook cards.

"We never have played cards before," Sarah say, showing thirty or forty of her baby teeth at once. "This is exciting."

Submariner husband nod head in agreement. Ms Puss hope neither of them have heart attack, for she feel responsible if so.

Finally, after Rook's eye glare like midnight goblin, Ms Puss and Oldcat give good-byes. Outside student apartments, still waving to turtle couple, Oldcat get in truck, wanting a drink so bad he drive straight to Brass Chimpanzee just like his pick-up running on green and yellow turtle track to same.

"Know what he told me?" Oldcat ask as they pull into the bar's parking lot. Ms Puss shake head. "He told me the only reason he was majoring in city planning was because Sarah was."

"She say same thing about him." Ms Puss inform Oldcat.

She and Oldcat laugh.

"Imagine: they'll have that same turtle thirty years from now, just in a bigger bowl."

Ms Puss nod at what Oldcat say and picture five-pound turtle blorping in tub, lounging near dinner table, watching Sarah and submariner husband eating dry meat loaf, instant mashed potatoes, and canned green beans. Whoa-ho! They accidental drop bean on turtle's head and it nod in excitement, opening its hooded eyes all of halfway.

Inside Brass Chimpanzee, Oldcat lift his beer and Ms Puss imitate the way he drink it, hooding her own eyes. *It's almost,* she think as she feel her spine tingle, *it's almost like I'm entering into olympic training to win the Guinness Record Book Competition as the world's longest turtle love.*

Want to know the thing that crawl just under Ms Puss's subconscious skin and frighten her the most? A voice, female or male, she cannot tell, calling, *Yes, dear, but just what is it that you'll win?*

The Compassionate X-ian

Oldcat, him and friend Tom decide a change of scenery might percolate their lives better than pure Columbian ground. So they, in their limited human capacity, drive to new bar called Far Away Places that rest in Carpenterville about as comfortable as a Buddhist shrine would in Jonesboro, Arkansas.

Oldcat and Tom both halt at door upon spotting tenderest bartender they ever see. Her face an oriental almond, her hair a cool black silk robe with tassels from Victoria's Secret, her full lips engendered and flourished to forever en-chant kinky lines from *Kama Sutra*, and her red dress, it flow as free and pure as blood of any innocent lamb.

Maybe Tom accustomed to this Oriental type beauty, for he only pause at door then walk on. His nonchalance come about no doubt because while Oldcat chasing college sportball in States and getting ready to wrench his back, Tom straight out of high school carrying ammunition rounds in Khe Sanh. . . . America, who ever doubt that it truly a land of multiple opportunity.

In fact, Viet vet Tom so non-nonplussed that him already at bar and ordering beer, just as if those Kama Sutra lips present most everyday sight in world, say "Pitch in" trash can or electronic door to small-town grocery store. Oldcat, though, he still stumbling on doorsill. Finally he wobble inside and warble his order to Thai lady.

He and Tom then sit at bar hour-so, while Mama-san demonstrate how Thai dancers bend fingers, show them Chinese exercise balls that cure both arthritis and Carpel computer syndrome, show them lastly a miniature silver buddha.

"Always must place this statue up high to show respect. Buddha, he just like Jesus, you know."

Oldcat leaning so far forward to watch Thai woman's beautiful hands, eyelashes, hips, and smile that he wonder if himself going to be converted on the spot, despite the fact that this silver buddha globbier than any Father God, more like Pillsbury Doughboy who been chrome-plated to act as talisman for driver's cab of front-lift dump truck.

Still, Oldcat leaning. If he do become converted, he wonder, how he ever explain to Ms Puss? *Those twins you carrying in your belly? We need to raise them to drink oolong tea and pray to Buddha.*

—Why, Oldcat?

—Because I go to bar and meet beautiful Thai woman who convert me, that why.

—Oh. Okay, Oldcat. Anything you say. You my so-wise, so-wonderful hero.

It no doubt probably not come down quite like that. Him better stick to skinny X-ianity and cross after all. He lean back from bar and tell tender oriental barwoman that he want to buy silver Buddha. He also promise to place it up high, like Jesus. Thai woman in silky red dress strut high heels back to closet to find gift wrap box. Tom, sitting next to Oldcat, raise skeptical Khe Sanh eyebrow, but Oldcat no mind.

"You gonna place that little statue of Buddha as high as her tits or her lips?" Tom whisper while looking at Thai woman, but watching Oldcat.

Oldcat fume. Sure enough, his motives may be mixed and impure like he a tiny man version of President Jimmy Carter lusting in mind, but at least he not chomping fried chicken, bamboozling old folks' money, seducing teenaged girls, and wailing sour milk lies over the airwaves like Southern televangelists. It too bad some X-ians no place Calvary Cross up high, where it belong.

Him just about to spout all this lonesome righteous drivel to friend Tom when Thai woman bend, and frilly red slip and lots of legs show—maybe in that order, who know? Not Oldcat, for his nose flare in such mindlust that he have to laugh at own self.

"Her eyes, Tom. As high as her eyes. That's where I'll place that fat Buddha. It's a damned sight farther than most X-ians ever get."

"Ah so. True enough, butterfly," Tom say. "My friend, let me buy you a drink. Maybe, just maybe, you'll make a good convert to the compassionate Buddha yet."

Marx, PC, and Camembert Cheese

Ex-jock Oldcat have friend entering into Ph.Deedom. Friend worried about gradual school and hinky professors, so Oldcat, who just get engineering degree and notification of new job in Alabama town, say, "They human same as you. Me read somewhere that shape of academics change, that most professors now come from lower middle class families. They understand tough times and real world. Relax, be yrself."

Before, at student parties, this friend be him Kentucky self 100 percent until the cows moo and red clover bloom, so Oldcat presume that action be no problem. But what this that happen? Oldcat think he detect tiny sniffling when he mention "lower middle class." Maybe friend catching cold.

Fourteen years later, Oldcat meet friend in Atlanta bar hotel, where they both attending separate conventions. In fact, Oldcat and Tom had picked up academic schedule of events just that morning and been burping coffee and laughing all day: "Here's a good one we should attend: 'Narcissism and the White Male, or Gutting Gender from the Classroom.' How they gonna do that? Cut off penises?" Tom want to know. "What about breasts, they remain okay, or PC police going to cut them and nipples off too?"

It happen that Tom and Oldcat in hotel bar, still snickering, when Oldcat spot friend and wave him over. Friend sit, talk for a while, then order Camembert cheese, Pouilly-fuisse wine, and spout so much PC correctum that Oldcat fear himself reverting to football animaldom, wanting to clothesline this penicilnecked weirdo professor. Him even notice that his spine hurt, he's thinking so much of tackling, grunting, and blocking.

Final wheat germ sprout when at end of *petite déjeuner* friend say, "Instead of dividing the check, each one of us can look at it and calculate what he or she ordered."

There be no she's sitting at table, just three he's: friend, Oldcat and Tom. Moreover, Oldcat sure this democratic nicety really appreciated by busy she waitress who have plenty other thing to do than stand by table and worry about tight academic getting pennies and pronouns right.

How this ever come about? This friend indeed from lower middle class family, just like article and statistics say. Oldcat know this for a fact. Oldcat even imagine what friend like in childhood: He buy tropical fish tank, breed guppies and swordtails, he collect grocery sacks of comics. "How smart Johnny be," his parents must have said. "Read all the time; then spend many hours thinking and watching fish." But just what do Johnny, with his big ears and little mean brain, really think all this time, Oldcat wonder. *Paugh on stupid poor parents? Me get more out of life? Me be professor and wear funny black hat with pastel tassel and gown with velvet stripes? Be silken just like royalty? That make up for these stupid guppies and swordtails? These stupid Mouse cartoon and Superman comic books? Paugh, me never again eat hamburger, but always nibble warm Camembert cheese that run in slow Loire valley streams like society ladies peeing between acts at civic opera*? Do him think all this and hate parents, hate all of neighborhood for being poor, for serving fish sticks on Friday and playing baseball on Saturday?

"Calculate what *he or she* ordered!? What? Someone have quick-artist sex change in bathroom?" No one really say this, but Oldcat know that waitress and Tom surely think it.

Waitress, she depend on tips, so she bite tongue and smile to Tom, who she been flirting with most successfully. Tom, he remain being polite-like to Oldcat's old friend and stare at large swollen hands instead of laughing aloud. Oldcat himself, he embarrassed and look up to TV, where a newscast cast ragged people begging in icy Moscow street. Him realize: American professors just like old partyliners in what was once USSR: inside Kremlin offices, they toasty warm, eat Camembert cheese and swill dyed cherries soaked in Dom Perignon champagne; outside, they bow-wow PC correctum and baby Marxism, when whole world longtime know: Marx he laid in snow-covered grave and dissolved gummier and moldier than any swank cheese.

And yes, there's a moral, Oldcat realize as he pull out wallet to pay bill: *Beware of old dogs who pretend to learn new tricks.*

Limbo

1.

"Miz Scahlet, I don't know nuttin about birthin babies!" Ms Puss laugh and say this to her daughter-in-law. They sitting on back porch, looking down on field full of cattle, and in the distance beyond, a swollen river tossing brown foam and broken tree limbs. It early summer, and heavy spring rains still muddying river, which dampen only some small bit the cookout announcement by Grrr and wife Michelle that she pregnant.

All family there, including Ms Puss's parents. Her dad roaring so happy and so loud about being great grandparent-to-be that she see Oldcat not so subliminally wish for cotton balls in ear—or in her dad's mouth, if they manufacture them large enough.

Meow's home too, taking a study break from her American history 4.0 G.P.A. at University of Alabama to visit. Ms Puss look away from dad and husband to spy her daughter through sliding glass door leading to kitchen. All the time, all the time, she think, she's getting more like her father and Oldcat's father too, the big Civil War buff, as he calls him. She'll probably soon start smoking imported cigars.

Meow turn and smile at her mom, then walk toward back door, with a wine cooler in hand, followed by brother Grrr who's carrying decaffeinated iced tea for the pregnant and careful Michelle.

"You're going to be next, Sis," he say.

Ms Puss pick up her ears.

"Oh no. Not yet. You and Michelle can have my next one. I'm entering law school in the fall."

Seeing her mother, Meow stop suddenly and grab her twin brother and pull him back to kitchen. It clear to Ms Puss that her daughter not mean to announce her acceptance into law school this evening, which belong to Grrr and Michelle. Ms Puss approve and turn back to Michelle.

"They no have sonograms when I had Meow and Grrr," Ms Puss is explaining as son and daugther leave kitchen through sliding glass door. "Oldcat and I knew we were going to have twins because of heartbeats, but that was about all."

"Couldn't even tell when one was going to be such a lunkhead as your husband," Oldcat interrupt, being on his third beer and in a four-squared happy mood. Ms Puss know that he decide to imitate her dad for cro-magon brashness—no doubt because he looking down on enough barbecuing chicken breasts for family, dogs and tribe of all twelve apostles too, if they care to drop by.

"He's no lunkhead," Dad-in-law shout from lounge chair, bunching dark eyebrows and rising to bait.

Ahh, family life, Ms Puss think, seeing Oldcat with simultaneity run same phrase on lips. Ms Puss smile quietly: it just like they star-crossed lovers from some S-peare play.

2.

. . . Six month, five day later, Ms Puss standing in hospital room with Michelle and Grrr, who been convinced to come in and support Michelle at delivery, despite his cracker Summons County upbringing.

Everything going fine until everything go wrong. Michelle get sharp stabbing pains, become clammy, and doctors have to cut baby out.

Abruptio Placentae. Baby not even get chance to see the world and how it run, before it tear loose and stop. And all the shiny machines, rushing nurses and shouting doctor-men not ever put its little gray tear together again.

Not even one hour later, Ms Puss standing by window in hall outside hospital room. She just now hear Grrr inside talking low, so Michelle must be coming out of anesthesia. Ms Puss hear Michelle's hoarse cry when she find out that infant die.

To Ms Puss, that cry sound like the creaking of old Mother Earth. She look out window: traffic along the street below snarled—it's evening rush hour in big burg of Carpenterville. *I been here before,* she think, leaning her forehead against the cool glass. *This just like looking over about-to-be-auctioned Thursday cattle happily roaming Wednesday field in back of house.* Then she remember that today is Friday. Of sudden, tears run down her cheeks, overflowing muddily onto her nose just like the Sucarnochee River did six months ago when they first stood on deck celebrating Michelle and Grrr's good news. Thinking of that evening, Ms Puss once again wring hands as if she were a wiry black woman playing bit part in Civil War film.

Little baby, little baby, she think. *What? You get premonition of the way things were and say no?*

Door click open and Grrr walk out of room. "Mom, she wants to hold it. Will they let her?"

Of this, Ms Puss herself not sure. "They may have . . . he may not . . ."

She already tell more than he know, for she heard nurses and doctor call infant a boy.

Grrr make face like Oldcat's Buddha that he so careful to keep high on wall for whatever reason, then he speak: "I know, Mom, but she wants to hold it. Will you tell them that?"

Ms Puss nod and spot confused moon hung outside when there still daylight straining to hold onto day. Maybe the baby's already up there looking down on us just like we're cattle on boggy land near muddy river, she think. Then she squeeze her son's hand and walk toward nurse's desk.

"We frown on that," a sharp-shouldered doctor there sure enough say, intruding on question Ms Puss asking nurse, using the royal *we* physicians trained to use like they have sole, blue-blooded claim to snoot. He then clip pink slip to a board with a commanding clack, but Ms Puss, she not even jump. Death already dam her way today: she certainly not going to be snagged by some dull-headed prick of a stump.

"That's stupid. Who play you to tell her what she wants? The girl may have hired you, doctor, but we paying the bill. You want to get paid instead of sued, you bring her her dead baby. Now."

3.

. . . How many months later it take for Ms Puss to laugh at herself as she relate this story to Oldcat? It come about on a Friday, when they sipping a special vintage year of wine from Japanese boss and debating whether to take a weekend camping trip: "You would have died, Oldcat.

I was just like my father, using his same 'That's stupid,' argument, gathering my brows with his same cave man intensity, like I was facing down a tree-god's thunderstorm." She pause to look down over Sucarnochee River, now running dry instead of muddy. She once read how fish hibernate for years in a dried river bed, unaware of their surroundings, to come to life whenever water returns. A Limbo of their own, so to speak.

Good Father Powers and all his thirty young years assured her and Michelle that his conditional baptism sent the baby straight to heaven, that the belief that unbaptized souls are forever lost and suspended motionless in Limbo was a thing of the past that the Catholic Church didn't adhere to anymore.

Still, Ms Puss think, looking down on neighbor's cows who've made it past one more Thursday auction, who are renting meadow space for at least one more week ahead; *still, there are times when a motionless Limbo doesn't seem all that bad a place to be.*

But just as quickly she smell Michelle's perfume, what she wore that baby-announcement day, even though Michelle's not there, but in Birmingham at what Oldcat call Mighty Miracle Mall shopping with Grrr.

You leave too, Ms Puss suddenly tell herself, looking down at the bone-dry river bank. *Leave, don't hibernate.* And though she know that there is water flowing, however slowly, somewhere out of sight, it seems much too fragile a trickle to ever force a blossom.

"A penny for your thoughts," Oldcat say, sniffing expensive wine and wrinkling nose.

Quaffing. Ms Puss smile at that word, shake her head and put down her fine wine glass with a clink. "I was thinking, Oldcat, that we should go ahead and leave for the lake tonight. We'll arrive just before dark and can set up a tent. It'll be rushed, but it'll be fun, won't it? A challenge that'll keep us hopping. We can finish the wine by our campfire."

Limbo, it seemed to Ms Puss, durated for ages and ages before Oldcat finally agreed.

Anatomy Lesson: Brain Stem

Oldcat, him stand in Oysterhead Lounge's quaint green rest room and pee, while having this one-way conversation with own nakedly dangling private anatomy:

"If you a real man, we go out back and fight right now."

No answer.

"But no, you too stupid to fight, huh?"

No answer.

"Not too damned stupid to slip wick into Ms Puss's own best good friend Jackie, though, huh?"

No answer.

"Why you no just go hotdog with Ms Puss's sister too? That be cute. Open American relish harem."

No answer, just dribbled pee.

"Maybe I wring you little neck like a rooster, finish your problem forever right now in this stinky bathroom that bartender Pat no clean for five long year."

No answer.

"What you getting swolled up for in here? You smell Jackie Babe perfume through bathroom wall? Want to peck out plaster hole to get a better sniff?"

No answer.

"You no listen to me, you no listen to Tom, you no listen even to Jackie, but you just had to get slick and see what her cave all about, huh?

"Maybe you listen to Sigfried Freud? We seance him here from grave, promise him a little cocaine snort and big Cuban cigar. Hep us, hep us, Mr Sir Herren Freud. Hep us, cause we so damned dumb we don't even know when our own pee wet."

There come a little squirt?

"Happy now, Spelunkite? Oh boy, you dribble big mess. You like a dog marking territory in fire hydrant plant. Me sorry you ever born. Say, how about me just leave you unzipped, so you can see what going on everywhere out there in barroom? But no, cause then me have to buy muzzle and rabies shot, yes? Otherwise I be sued."

No answer.

"Hey, how many time we going to have this conversation, anyway?"

"*Lots.*"

Oldcat, him no even jump. Hell, drippy dumb dick doing all the thinking for him up to now: it might as well speak.

How Come?

Oldcat driving to work in rain, fumble-thinking about coming weekend; Ms Puss already left for class at JC half an hour before, so she probably want to study most of tomorrow. *Ms Puss, she be real enough nurse soon, and that make her happy, so that make me happy, yes?* Oldcat ask self.

Oldcat slow car on seeing black people gathered ahead near tiny rural bridge. He see that they all staring down a fifteen-foot embankment. He also see a police car parked before bridge with its blue lights lazing, with its policeman standing in orange rain slicker outside, sputtering on radio. Policeman, he a deputy sheriff that Oldcat no know. In fact, Oldcat no know anyone gathered here, though he often enough swear he know everyone in Summons Count—

—That silver-gray car look—

Oldcat feel saliva catch in throat, feel stomach swell.

He pull off into mud and walk back, him shoes picking up wet clay just same as his heart picking up voltage from snappish overcast sky.

Him stop—bang!—and focus on mud-streaked mirror of overturned car in deep ravine: it a dull black plastic like Ms Puss's Nissan. He feel heart pump. Them clothes in back, though—they not ours, are they? But Ms Puss did go to Wal-Mart yesterday and there lies a crumpled Wal-Mart bag—Hey! No! Everybody go to Wal-Mart, Oldcat assure self. Pound-pound, bash-bash go his heart, jerking out voltage enough for three overnight thunderstorms.

Black men all staring.

Oldcat staring.

Deputy the only person talking, and that on rubber ducky two-way.

Oldcat feel right foot urging rest of body to walk down rain-wet slope, when he hear two-way screech: "Uh, the registered owner of your charcoal Toyota sedan is a Miss uh Jacqueline Hudson of 435 Rose Street, Carpenterville—Ten-four?"

Everybody standing still except Oldcat: him feel electricity drain from his wet shoes into ground, him feel his eyes nervously watering as he sludge back to car, still too sick to be either happy or relieved that this Miss uh Jacqueline Hudson yet one more person in Summons County he not know.

Him pull out of mud and drive along road, trying to spy sun peeking through after rainstorm. It percolating there somewhere, he know, along with maybe a rainbow. *I love Ms Puss, soon-to-be registered nurse. I truly love her. I love her, love her, love her! Study tomorrow, Ms Puss, tonight we go out and Friday-celebrate like we never done before. Never before.*

I love her, lover, lover.

Oldcat love her so much that him feel a tumor growing tendrils from his stomach to his heart, taking nourishment from all the ozone left in that same area.

Love her, love her, love her.

How come, he think, passing a wrecker with blinking yellow caution lights, *that it take such a sad, stupid thing as an overturned silver-gray automobile to make me realize something so very happy, so very smart?*

Saturdays

A Tisket, a Tasket

Oldcat, he travel with friend Tom on a convention trip to Washington D.C., where-there they forage on fancy ethnic food to learn Worldly and Charming, salute N.R.A. Building in case any patriotic Alabama spies are watching, give homeless people pocket change to buy whatever make them happy in their brief journey, and of course, drink and drink until partyland clock indicate no more.

One unconventional morning, Oldcat decide him actually will attend a meeting, so him noose a tie about his throat and don a dandy thin coat with threads barely enough to tassel bottom stripe of Betsy Ross's flag, much less flap away cold December wind that pound hard immediate upon him stepping from revolving hotel door.

When him try to stick chaffed hands in threadbare pockets, moreover, he discover that some stupid tailor sew them closed to create the sleek, executive look. *Monsieur, monsieur, what gentle businessman ever soil his finely tailored suit with notes, money, schedules or other hoi polloi manure, manure?*

Despite this ice-cubed inconvenience, Oldcat ball fists and hike toward next hotel and its early morning meeting, entitled, "Managing Employee Grievances," subtitled, "When To Give In, and When To Squelch the Whim." He chewing lips at title and walking brisk and curious in cold D.C. wind like naive Southerner him is, when of sudden, not even two block gone along, a gallumphing stilty weirdo wearing a thirteen-pocket army trenchcoat call parade halt on freezy sidewalk to salute Oldcat—one uniform to another. No tailor sew up *those* pockets, cause all thirteen stuffed with bus schedules, rocks, sardine cans, dimestore jewelry, used stamps, bottle openers, Bic lighters, string and twine, tiskets and taskets. As Oldcat gawk and weirdo stand salute-still, a dirty mouse trap fall out. *My sweet Lord. This tall weirdo some escaped anal retentive or a What?* Oldcat wonder.

A What, he decide, for weirdo ignore fallen mousetrap and keep smile while saluting, his cheeks as Puritan and barnyard sallow as American Gothic, his nose as red as old-liner Wobbly commie. Seeing all those yellow peril teeth grinning up there so heightsome in winter headwinds whipping from surrounding nine-story buildings Oldcat too have to smile. He even click heels and salute back: it a patriotic duty.

"Al-l-ll right! That's six!" Weirdo clap ragged gloves in muffled sound and announce this to surrounding buildings like he Julie Andrews preparing to pop umbrella and fly. Then he slump for mousetrap, pop back up and haul his thirty-two yellow teeth and his thirteen greenly bulging pockets glawking down the street, legs strutting like drumsticks of some fly turkey who been hunkering at Hidden Swamp and so survive chopping block for one more Thanksgiving Day.

Six? That's six? Oldcat numbly echo while he watch thirteen pockets turn a corner like the original colonies skipping nursery rhymes around a maypole. *Six?* What happen when lanky weirdo hit seven? Him kick mousetrap into air, pull Uzi, greased and neatly folded, from largest pocket and blast away?

But then Oldcat hear another "All-right!," another muffled clap of hands echoing from around corner, breaking cold morning air. He blow warm breath into hands and walk on, chiding self: Oldcat, say-if your two threadbare pockets ever do rip open, you nowhere near imaginative enough to homestead streets as a larky What—you only anal enough to stuff them and retend. Oldcat, Oldcat, it such a wonderful brisk morning, and that thirteen pocket salute breezing about so carefree, full, and happy. Zazen blow all your negative paranoia juices out into D.C.'s winter air. Go drink your acidic coffee, go eat your greasy donut, go attend your boring meeting. Meanwhile, open your eyes to the globular world and don't be jealous of pure freedom just cause some high-toned tailor sewn shut the only two pockets in your own dandified coat.

Oldcat sniff air jauntily and walk on, passing D.C. trash and circulars flapping in street. Of sudden he spy seven beads of a broken amber necklace lying near garbage can. He stoop and pick them up, sniff at chill blue sky, then stuff them in pants pocket with money clip and change. Pocahontas jewels from Smithsonian! He kick heels and clap his bare hands sharply to shout, "All right!"

The Non-tological Argument

Oldcat, him and friend Tom bachelor-visit Stone Mountain. From car, they sight-see into distance: "Ugh, granite top loom so ugly it almost pretty, like bald girlfriend this friend of mine once had," Oldcat say.

Tom, he smile sly and nod.

Traffic so there-much sprawl that they have to join about-in-on, like crazed cattle, only to gyre circles into more circles and more, until finally they dizzily desert car in parking lot pen, gaze up at mountain (still ugh!), step over dead chew tobacco wad not yet rigor-mortised, kick six seven beer or pop can of various brand out of way, and sneeze at pine needles.

Thenupon as if not enough, Tom stick left front foot in Hotlanta chew gum. . . .

They brave even then to laugh, but how long that ability persist in this messy Dixie sun?

But not six steps around a row of pine trees . . . boom-soon! The park jump-start to life with old ladies to wag under blue hair; kids to scamper like their snotty gray noses magically hot-wired to blue overhead sky; reddlenecks to waddle until brains canter toward ivory beer belly; Southern belles to sway with ding-dong brains glued under puffball hair poised greenly-bleachy for catching in ceiling fan and splatting white lice about the ballroom floor. . . . All these and more multi-colored denizens come to emerge from Hotlanta haze left by Sherman one hundred ten thousand year ago. Invasion of Brain Snatchers to the fore.

"They not tourists. What they do here?" ask Tom, swishing tail anxiouslike, pointing out the many Georgia Peach license plates. What? He back-flashing to firefight night on Khe Sanh?

Oldcat answer, "Honor Confederate dead, wish it still live? Finalize etiquette for crawling under hoop skirts? Snort snuff, brandish Rebel battle flag at passing blacks, slurp Coca-Cola, misspell household words to prove beyond doubt they Southern? Got me, Brother Tom, I don't know."

Clanga clang!

Come around manicured bend this miniature choo-choo with red-faced conductor who memorize every player on Hotlanta Braves, Hawks, *and* Falcons too, you bet. But can he drive choo-choo? Paranoia spreading from Tom and Oldcat gather its fear: much steam in boiler, red-faced conductor may craze own self with heat, hallucinate that he running down disruptive Freedom Riders from North.

Denizens around Oldcat and Tom, though, they not worry: they whoop and board train. Oldcat and Tom look at one another, lay ears back, sprint across narrow gauge track while red-faced conductor busily engage self in a genteel Southern burp. Safe . . . unless conductor know how to jump avenging train from track. Just in case that so, Tom make quick motion with thumb as whistle blow, and they hustle-hike up perceived safety of Stone Mountain.

This mountain: it got rock, it got scrub pine, it got leftover white trash, it got hot. What else it got? It got two tired hepcats named Oldcat and Tom, walking up its side. Halfway, they sit on wood bench, observe wasps and one ant tumble into soft drink can. Observe screambo boy and girl twirl one another like mad electrons in spin. Where parents? Who know, who care? This modern day America, remember.

"We go on up?" ask Oldcat.

Tom, he nod. Train conductor still rebel-shouting below, and anything to get away from mid-mountain screambos and wasps, for Tom develop allergies to both. So trudge on they do, until even pine trees get sick of fighting rock and let Georgia's bald geology hang out.

"My god-who-does-exist, this mountain certainly ugly," Oldcat say.

Breeze come, hot and nasty, bearing sulfurous odor in a dirty, squeak-wheeled wheelbarrow. It whirl over Oldcat and Tom, then actually droop like banshee to speak: "Yes, mortal, you right: this mountain uglier than gutsick buzzard. Me been think that for oh-so long whenever me come passing over—so why all these people up here now do climb? Why *you* up here do climb?"

"STEP RIGHT THIS WAY!" Loudspeaker voice rudely interrupt un-natural speaking phenom.

Oldcat turn and sniff: That smell, it not sulfur . . . it Southern pork bar-b-que—how could he have ever confused the two?

"My god-who-must-exist," he intone, "would you look at that ugly concrete rectangle perched on top of this ugly stone hill. It almost like it grew here from stone seed. Tom, we must walk up, go in to believe, yes-no?" Tom nod, as perplexed as Prometheus burning an innocent forefinger.

Once they stand inside the concrete rectangle, more screambo kids, blue-haired ladies, drooling potbellies, boring-a-ding Southern belles—whole 97 technicolor yards shimmer from bland concrete walls to confront Oldcat and Tom. Tom, he tremblingly point outside, through several plate glasses, toward assembly line of denizens belching from cable car that recently tumbled up the far side of mountain, what been hidden from their view before.

It make sense enough that this mountain have two maybe even more side, but these denizens . . . brrr. They one and all and each same-side toddle toward concrete rectangle wherein Oldcat and Tom now standing, no doubt to search for singlebrained infusion of sugar and hog grease.

"My god-who-might exist," Oldcat pray. "So this where they all come from. Georgia mass-producing them, just like Detroit defect autos. They like Barbie and Ken dolls, only part missing is plastic brain that squirt pink water."

Tom, meanwhile, mimic motion of stuffing hamburger in mouth, patting belly.

"Hah," he exclaim. "By your god-who-should-exist, it's a wonder that cable don't snap from carrying all the extra pork rind and bar-b-que ribs back down. If it did, it might even be a disguised bless—"

"SHOWTIME IN TEN MINUTES!" the loudspeaker voice interrupt.

Turning around, Tom and Oldcat spot a bronze plaque on the wall, then walk to read it:

> The Ku Klux Klan was founded here
> on a stormy night in 1915,
> when they offered prayers
> through the dark
> under a lightning-lit cross.

Prayers? Tom back-paddle away, fearing bolt from blue sky going to sizzle through grease exhaust and blast bronze plaque and concrete base for blasphemy.

"They brag at that? They pray? They happy?" Oldcat ask.

"Varroooooooom!" shout denizen scampering over polished tile gripping pork rib in its mouth, barbecue sauce slinking down cheeks like battle-gore.

The two friends leave the building. Oldcat shield eyes from all the surrounding so-ugly. A teenage belle in a pastel pink hoop-dress push a flier toward Tom and shout, "Y'all come to thuh lasur show toniiiight? It's gonna show Gen-ruhl Lee, Stone-wahl Ja-ickson and Presuh-dent Jaiff Davis just like when they wuz aliiive."

Behind belle, cable car lurch to spew more beaming Barbie and Kens. Where their brains, where?

Oldcat blanch, wiping belle's spittled Southern syrup from his face. He and Tom shake heads to refuse flier, then walk to mountain's edge and lamentate, like suffering children of Israel facing expansive desert:

"My god-who-cannot-exist, why have you forsaken us? They claim you create heaven and earth in one week. Paugh! Why you no take pride and be a craftsman, take thousands of years like Darwin want? Just look at this mess! Must have been rush order birthday present to Satan you was working on. No other excuse to so bungle job."

What answer they expect from mountain and any nearby supernatural phenom? The same as do we all:

"I so sorry, little pilgrims. Place new work order in triplicate and upgrade come UPS overnight from St. Pete and Gabriel right away."

What answer they get?

None-bone, none-bone, none-bone . . .

Star of Bethlehem

Oldcat and Ms Puss been married ten years when this particular Christmas come. Since children out in den marking toy-store catalogues with wish-list hints, he and Ms Puss sit to coffee-drink at kitchen table, looking out toward field empty of cows this morning. Maybe they all sweeping stable for to kneel and worship on Christmas Eve, who know, who can tell?

"What you doing?" Oldcat ask, lifting eyebrow like Jack Nicholson starring in X-mas thriller about slasher-Santa hopping through famous Toronto underground Mall.

"Sending Christmas cards out."

"Ah. But why mark with pencil in book?"

"I check these people we're sending a card. When they send one back, I circle their name. No circle for two year, no more check, but big black X."

"Big black X? You mean you don't send them anymore card?"

"That my smart Oldcat."

Oldcat glance under table to see if Ms Puss wear ugly wicked Witch of West Boots. No, she have on silly reindeer slippers from last Christmas.

"You think that show proper spirit of Season?" he ask, looking away from reindeer slippers to glum, dark X forming on address book, just like slow cancer spotting smoker's lung.

"They no care 20 cent stamp about us, why we care about them?"

"You sound like A-rab and Jew, like Soviets and Whattheirnames, like —"

"Like geography of whole planet. . . . Oldcat, since whendate you elected blind seer and climb in Ivory Tower—you no professor."

In strut daughter Meow with catalogue. "Me want this toy, this, this, that, that, hereone and thereone," she say, standing on her mother's reindeer slipper.

Oldcat close eyes and try to imagine cold night and Star of Bethlehem: instead, he only envision hot Arab-like desert and fat iron bomb perched rickety atop Los Alamos Trinity test tower. He once read that hotshot professor-scientists there place bet that first A-bomb no work, or that if it do, it cause chain reaction and disintegrate atmosphere of entire world. But Optimistheimer, that man knew it work, all right. So too did high-cheeky townsfolk of Nagasaki and Hiroshima. And Edward Teller? Him no give tinker's damn about dinky A-bomb; him plan H-bomb to stink like world never seen. Oldcat tremble: far too many exploding stars crowding out Bethlehem inside closed eyes. Why those hotshot professor scientists name their test bombing Trinity, like it immediate inheritor to Godhead?

"Honey, you can't have all those toys. Pick three, and if Santa can find them in his workshop, you'll get them."

That report come from Ms Puss. Oldcat forget H-bomb, A-bomb, Arabs and Star of Bethlehem to watch her and Meow cuddle at table. Ms Puss busy teaching Meow to make check-marks and circles and mean black X's on Christmas card list.

Maybe Optimistheimer right with Trinity: maybe that terrible flash what the Star of Bethlehem really all about. Noel, noel; blow to hell, blow to hell. Let both charity *and* hate begin at home. Oldcat feel giddy as daughter Meow lick lip and press to imprint a very dark X. Him search table for sports pages so to escape into StupidWorld, but him need rattle paper only once to smell Terrible T Truth rising over coffee, donut crumbs and dead-rose vase: of course, go ahead and print the *X* in X-mas, where it belong anyoldway. Him glad his twin children have wise mother who teach them how well to get along in this world.

. . . Really, him glad.

One Never-Ending Plot

For long time, Oldcat and Ms Puss have two married friends named John and Melody.

"You know," Ms Puss once say, "we never seen them fight. Isn't that wonderful?"

Oldcat snap back: "They probably divorce next year." Maybe him thinking of self and past girlfriend who sudden leave him for Gainesville lawyer—she never bother to argue, she just gone. Or maybe him eat too much vanilla ice cream last night, of consequent his genes gum up and today throw out aberrant, cynical pheromes. Or maybe, just just just maybe, him thinking of recent Labor Day fling-ding with Jackie Babe and projecting on own self and future Marriage Encounter. Halloween come soon and he may wear scary mask in more way than one because of *that* ridiculous affair, he fear.

Ms Puss snort at Oldcat's reply and walk into kitchen to roar garbage disposal way past empty. Oldcat wince, thinking of him peter stuck in disposal and him self howling; onlooking Ms Puss and Jackie Babe both be howling too, but for vastly merrier reason. . . .

Two weeks later, who come for barbecue but John and Melody. Melody, she so dark and beautiful with her Italian skin; John, him like miniature Paul Bunyan.

"If they ever redo the American Gothic," Tom say, opening a beer can as the couple we speaking of de-car in Oldcat's back yard, "they should paint those two to give us Carpenterville peons something to ooh and admire."

"What's the 'American Gothic'?" Oldcat ask.

"You sure you went to college? Yeah, that's right, you played football."

Oldcat ignore remark and flip hamburgers, noticing that John carrying six pack of St. Pauli Girl up driveway, Melody swinging two Sprite, one in each hand like go-away-snake club. It been this way since time prehistoric, him think, imagining couples riding baby brontosaurus over to neighborly cave for food and drink. . . .

Soon after modern-day sun toss off its last ultraviolet burbles, all five eaten enough grease that they indeed start to grunt indecipherable cave talk. Oldcat even feel canine teeth glint as moon rise, and him wonder where Meow and Grrr are. Better not be at this place, better not be at that place. . . . They for sure *some* place in his new car. Him pause and open another beer, thinking that at least they couldn't have wrecked a baby brontosaurus: ahh, those were good old days.

"Don't you think you've had enough?" Melody ask when John eye nearly empty fifth beer.

Oldcat guiltily jump, thinking she mean him; then him ears prick up. *Drink only male bastion left after so much feminist wagtalk. Now, Ms Puss, you watch: we gonna see male war dance, no more love-dove.*

But John actually wink at Melody—a huge enough wink that Oldcat can spy it by the Citronella flame. "I suppose you're right. We have things to do at home, don't we?" Then him turn to Ms Puss, Oldcat, and Tom: "Tomorrow is our tenth wedding anniversary." Him pause, "But it's tonight that we're going to take the cruise—straight to the romantic South Sex Seas."

Ms Puss gulp her Manhattan and laugh. Melody slap husband's arm. "I can't believe you're so vulgar to say that in front of our friends."

At this, John open sixth beer while Melody sip second Sprite.

Now argument come? Oldcat wonder.

But no, for soon happy giggle-couple drive off on motorized brontosaurus, leaving Oldcat, Tom, and Ms Puss to douse the Cave's Sacred Fire. As Oldcat roll sacrificial grill under overhanging deck, him gaze at nearly full moon and think of Jackie Babe, even as he hear Ms Puss upstairs humming song about love. Him then see Tom picking up trash from cookout campfire. Funny, but he never even yet told best friend Tom about Jackie Babe and Labor Day. . . . Afraid? Of course.

"See, Oldcat?" Ms Puss call down from window: "I told you so. They *still* haven't argued."

"Ha." Oldcat manage to answer.

Yes, that so, him think as night shift itself about his shoulders, *they really not argue. Maybe we remaining three should roll out grill and offer sacrificial dead cow meat and garlic salt to the glowing moon. After all, it surely constitute a sacred religious experience to encounter at least one plot that never ever end.*

Ellipsis

John and Melody, the couple who never argue, come to early Spring barbecue at Oldcat and Ms Puss's. Friend Tom, he there with hotshot date from Oysterhead; two other supervisors and wives from factory there; and also three friends of Ms Puss and their husbands, one being principal of high school. Jackie Babe, though, she call Ms Puss and say she sick and not able to come—what she tell Oldcat, he hope to keep state secret, even if Israeli Mesad torture him.

Overall, evening so beautiful warm, dead meat cook so crinkle-hot, smoke waft so odiferous in air, beer and drinks splash so icy cold, and children either so far away at babysitters or so busy planning senior prom that God surely do exist, all barbecuers think.

But within one hour, Doubting Thomas un-miracle occur. John and Melody argue.

Need to make this clear: Oldcat and Ms Puss been married eleventy year and *never* see this couple argue. All of Carpenterville say the same: this be model couple, should pose on cover of *Good Housekeeping*, maybe even as Team of Year for *Sports Illustrated.*

But tonight, one medium-rare hamburger splat and one plate drop on concrete patio, and either *J* or *M*—everyone too shocked to be sure—yell out at either *M* or *J*: "Clumsy ass!"

Whoever, whatever, both more embarrassed than proverbial uninvited wedding guest who gorge on too many flatulent pork 'n' beans, so both the two finish beer and Sprite and trundle home early, one five steps in front of other.

Three days later, Ms Puss hear through grapevine that John and Melody been try to have baby, and that Melody spot and lose pregnancy.

Ms Puss relate this to Oldcat, who put mouth in high gear and reply, "*That* explain it all. That just go to show . . ."

Sad to say, it just go to show so many things that Oldcat feel like clinging vine trying to grow up granite hillside. *How I ever finish this, my stupid, pretentious sentence,* him think. *Of course, same inane way, no doubt, that I finish life . . . with tiny ellipis of breath. It just go to show that ellipses were invented to honor some very quiet, though very sacred and significant unknown god.*

Double-entry Accounting

Oldcat and Ms Puss buy their twins Easter chicks. Two neighborhood dogs frisk into garage Saturday morning and all chicks massacred. Oldcat want to inform twins that chicks rise again, but X-ianity take it sad self too serious for that. No animal have soul.

Ms Puss, eternal smarts in house, suggest that Oldcat bury chicks while she drive to feed store and buy more. "Just like double-entry accounting, Oldcat. If you take them out of one column, put them in another."

Oldcat carry feathers, beaks, and bones to far back yard behind weeping willow to bury. While trying to keep digging a secret and watching Nintendo-playing children's window, he hear Ms Puss drive off. Was it with the thirteenth spadeful that he remembered her comment about double-entry accounting? No matter, for he remembered also that the founder of double-entry accounting was a thirteenth century monk named Pacioli. When Oldcat a young college thing, he was shocked to learn same—what any holy man doing thinking like that? Now, though, him not so cocksure. If X-ian god inspire monk to work in both black and red ink, maybe X-ian god take care of these little chick souls no matter what preacherman say.

Oldcat whistle "Rock of Ages" and feel giddy.

Next Saturday, him get phone call that father die.

In shock, him pull down suitcase from broiling attic over garage while Ms Puss arranging airline flights. Below, through thin ceiling that him always afraid going give way every time he crawl into lobster attic, he hear replacement column of chicks happily peeping behind their protective wire cage, despite that Easter and Resurrection done come, done gone.

All this prove why so much of world always remain non-Christian, him decide, gripping hot suitcase and feeling sweat drip from nose. Double-entry accounting, it fine for pocketbook and mind, but it entirely too much for human heart.

Hoof-and-Mouth

Ms Puss been sitting home thinking. This always, always bad news, Oldcat warn Meow and Grrr, who in junior high school and close to transforming into Teenaged Monsters from Black Lagoon, though their glands and gills only half-formated, so Oldcat still occasionally able to communicate.

"Your mother been spending so much time worrying about you, you, and me. She need time to worry about self now." Oldcat taste him spittle and think he wise as Solomon when he speak this to Meow and Grrr one night, simultaneous as local newscaster finish batting him-slash-her unisex eyes at TV-land viewers. Grrr busily remote clicking channel, but Oldcat retain great hope he still listen to Dad's Solomon like advice.

Next evening, Meow at least prove that she listen, for she meet with brother and father to show three books borrowed from school library to revitalize mom: one a philosophy text called *Ethics and the Contemporary Person,* one a classic called *Emma,* and one a strange book about reshaping America and the whole world through diet. "How Your Food Choices Affect Your Health, Happiness and the Future of Life on Earth!!" this book's back cover boldly, religiously proclaim.

"Tall carry-out order with all them capital letters and fat exclamation points," Oldcat comment.

"Oh. Ms Wright gave me that one," Meow inform her father and Grrr, who cautiously approving her selections. Daughter Meow dutifully place the books on kitchen counter where Ms Puss always work, taping an excellent-penmanshiped note to them that read, "For You, From Us, With Love."

More capitols, Oldcat think, but him not say anything. Instead all three hang about stairway peeping that evening until Ms Puss read the note and finger the books like they mousetraps. Then she step out of sight, hidden by the kitchen wall. She carrying them to secret lair? She gonna read them there? Gonna eat them? Burn them? Oldcat, Meow, and Grrr shrug shoulders at one another.

Five days later, family sit down to red beans and rice dinner.

"This make a great change," Oldcat say. Grrr and Meow slurp like incredible praying manta ogling creeping ten-legged innocents—which action seem to mean that they agree.

For dinner Tuesday night, family have Chinese-looking dish. "This make a great change," Oldcat say, not exactly stunning family with innovative conversation.

"What're these white chunky things?" Grrr ask.

"Tofu. It has all the protein of meat, but none of the cruelty."

Grrr upturn lips. "What's it made of?"

"Soured soybean curds, from soybean milk." Ms Puss smile.

Oldcat notice Meow make small grimace, like she embarrassed. What to be embarrassed about bean curds, he wonder, taking bite.

That night, he remember what Ms Puss say about "none of the cruelty." Cruelty? He turn to ask her what she meant, but she asleep already and him remember so-wise self-Solomon dictum and leave her to her dreams.

On Wednesday, family unit eat split pea soup and carrots with homemade zucchini bread. Oldcat force smile, twins force smile. On Thursday they eat chick-pea loaf with broiled pimento. Oldcat force smile, twins force smile.

"You have new cookbook?" he ask. Ms Puss just nod. Oldcat notice that Grrr later leave house and come back in one hour. He sniff reentering son for drugs and alcohol, smell only cheeseburger. Him want to say, "Next time buy me one," but bite tongue. Oldcat surprised at good taste therein. And why not? Tongue be the closest to meat he eaten in seven days.

Next night Friday. It getting warm and cookout weather, so Oldcat call from office and ask if Ms Puss want him to pick up four steaks.

"No, I have dinner planned. It's a surprise."

For rest of day, Oldcat drift through work, thinking of Meow's grimace on Tuesday night, Ms Puss's strange words that same night, and the surprise dinner coming up this night. Some strange revolt astir in his own kingdom, he fear.

That evening, they have spaghetti alfredo. But wait, this not real spaghetti even, not to mention real fettucine. Maybe Alfredo, he at least somewhere hiding in pot.

"It's spaghetti squash," Ms Puss say after they take their first bite and all look up. "It's spaghetti squash alfredo."

"Where's the meatballs?" Grrr ask.

Ms Puss sigh like she trying out for lead in S-peare drama. "This household no longer going to thrive on poor innocent tortured cows." She push away from table and go to counter and retrieve library book hidden behind bread bin.

Ahh, that's where she keeps them, rest of family think, exchanging glances.

"Look," Ms Puss say. "This is what you're really eating when you eat steak. Do you want to face responsibility for that at the dinner table every night?" She showing picture of tiny calf squished in torture chamber stall, wide-eyed with fear just like the evil hammer man who done bash six-seven nearby brethren has stopped outside its stall to smoke unfiltered cigarette, grin and wipe his sweaty hands on the bloody sledgehammer handle in relaxation.

"Ugh, close it, Mom. Take it away, please," Meow plead.

"No, turn it sideways," Grrr yell. "That calf reminds me of my last blind date."

"THAT not funny!"

Oh-oh. Ms Puss's screech not funny either. Yes indeed, palace revolt astir, Oldcat think. But who ever heard of queen leading it?

Family war council come Saturday morning in yard, after traditional sausage, pancakes and eggs spindle into whole wheat muffins and Egg-beaters.

"Dad, you're the man—can't you just order her to stop?"

Oldcat grimace at macho logic: Grrr only fourteen and already lived in Alabama too long.

"Mom's got rights too," Meow shout, stomping peat around rose bush like she readying it for brother's shallow grave.

"All right, all right," Oldcat admonish. "We need to work together in this. United we stand, divided we fall." He turn to his daughter. "What's happen now with your mother anyway?"

"It's that book I gave her from the school library. The one Miss Wright suggested. Miss Wright's a vegan."

"A what?"

"A vegan, a strict vegetarian. She won't eat meat, cheese, eggs, or any animal products at all. She says it's immoral."

"That's stupid," Grrr say, employing his grandfather's favorite argument. Oldcat not know whether to nod or shush his son, so he just ignore him as Meow explains more. . . .

"Okay," Oldcat finally tells Meow. "You the one to get us all out of this. First, you have your mom take you for a driving lesson today in the country. Go along Hwy. 45; there's no traffic and there's plenty of happy cows grazing in the fields, none of them in torture chamber stalls like she showed us in that damned book last night at supper."

"What do I tell her?"

"Tell? You've got her genes *and* mine—that means you smarter than us both. You'll figure out something. Tell her we're a growing family, that we need protein; tell her that we can't hold any more of our fun family grill-outs—"

"Tell her we'll all file for divorce," Grrr say, busting up peat moss from sack. "Hey! If we didn't have cows, how could we have this stuff?" he ask, looking down at sack.

"Peat moss is from trees, manure's from cows," Meow correct.

Grrr he just sulk. "It's not my fault. Can't nobody think right without meat."

. . . Five hours later, Ms Puss and Meow pull into driveway. It three o'clock in afternoon, and they begin unloading groceries. Oldcat and Grrr come in from den to help, grin and elbow one another on seeing packages of hamburger and chicken on counter.

"It worked, didn't it?" Oldcat whisper, giving his daughter a hug as Ms Puss walk back outside.

"Yeah, but not like you think. I drove to where you told me. But I ran off the road and scratched the car pointing out some cows to Mom. So then she insisted we drive to a different road where there weren't any cows and I could concentrate on my driving. But on that road were all these poor people's houses we kept passing, with no paint and all that stuff you see around here in town. Mom kept staring out the window, and when she finally took over driving again, we drove straight to the grocery. 'You can tell your father and brother that I'm going to save cows, chickens, and pigs for later,' she said. 'Maybe even my next incarnation. There's too many unhappy poor *people* in Summons County for a person to be worrying about animals.'"

Oldcat clap his hands and laugh, but Meow shake her head and continue as he unload a grocery bag full of meat that Grrr bring in. "So Dad, she's going to join a volunteer organization at the church to help poor people fix their houses, and I'm going to have to cook once a week."

Oldcat and Grrr have a big haw, Oldcat even bite brown bag to quiet himself so wife won't hear.

"Don't be so smug, Dad. While I'm home cooking dinner, you and Grrr are going to be out in the county helping fix those houses. Once a week, every Thursday.—That's what she said."

Oldcat stare at three-pound package of hamburger bleeding hot-pinkly on his hand. Thanks to USDA food inspectors, he not have to worry about hoof-and-mouth disease—but that irrelevant, for he feel sadly certain that him just contract a capital case of foot-in-mouth.

The Multiplication of Loaves

Oldcat, one Saturday morning while sun still nodding, wake to hear thump, thump, sounding through house like castle walls being besieged. What? She so tired of teenaged male friends of Grrr gulping hamburgers that she slaughtering own cow? Him dress in wife's robe and trot into kitchen where him find Ms Puss hitting at pile of dough. The way she turn and glare at him, then slap at bread, not make for good omen.

Sudden, Ms Puss roll dough into small bat, then hurl. Oldcat stagger, surprised how heavy lumped bread can be.

"Take *that* to Jackie Babe, why don't you, if she needs a prick so bad."

Oh this not going to be good day at all, Oldcat think, clutching at robe and dough denting his chest. Altogether, he feel like he about to be driven toward Golgotha.

"And don't you dare ask me 'What do you mean?' We both damned well know exactly what I mean."

Yes, we know, Oldcat think. "I'm sorry," he manage to say.

"Sorry." Ms Puss spit out word like it vinegar on sponge. "How could you? How could she? My best friend. My husband."

Oldcat squeeze doughbat against chest. It seem homey now and all that he's got, like a run-over puppy that he love. "We drunk one night at Oysterhead Lounge—" him never hear his voice so low, so low that it sound like George Kennedy or Jack Palance, so low that it pipewrench his throat.

"Oysterhead. What an appropriate name that place has." Ms Puss's fingernails dig into another loaf of dough. "Let me guess: someone filtered an aphrodisiac through the air-conditioning. You couldn't either of you help yourselves. And did you talk about me while you pawed her tanning salon body? Compare notes? Laugh?"

"Jackie cried afterwards. I felt sick."

"Sick. I bet. Just like you make me now. Sick."

Oldcat start to say, 'Hush, wait until the kids leave house,' but he remember they both staying at friend's lake cottage, getting into who knows what.

"You two have crucified me, just like the Jews."

Why everybody pick on Jews? Christ one too.—Maybe that's why, cause they crucified their own. Maybe Jews' big mistake was doing in public what everyone else do at home. Oldcat's mind irrelevantly-relevantly race onward.

"Sorry," he say again. "It's over. We've not see one another for five week now."

"Five weeks. So pained that you're counting the minutes, Oldcat? That's supposed to make me feel good? And how long did you *see* one another before that? A year? Two years? Since our trip to St. Augustine?"

"No! It wasn't anywhere near that long . . . just . . . some months," Oldcat say, hearing his voice plumb even lower, casting for rock-bottom of Snake River in Grand Canyon. He remember exact date, even, Labor Day, but damned if he stupid enough to say that now.

Another unbaked loaf come flying at him, and he catch this one to hold both ridiculously close to himself, false bosoms.

"Speak up! I want to hear the truth!" Ms Puss yell.

Oldcat, him think of Pilate jesting, "What is Truth?" Only reason Pilate could laugh and joke like Bob Hope was he didn't have to hang around for an answer. And Jesus, God save me, who did hang on the cross, was soon resurrected. So what hope left for little me and Bob?

Nonetheless, Oldcat tell the truth, at least as much as humans can bear. "It happen this way . . ." he begin blurily.

And lo! A miracle! After three hours of arguing and heaving and crying, Ms Puss produced another loaf from who-knows-where and hurled it at him, snapping his head heavily back into the refrigerator with such force that he fell. True to the Sermon on the Mount's admonition to 'Love thy neighbor,' she ran to steady him, and the two of them held one another in briny, doughy charity.

"It be okay. I'm sick and sorry," Oldcat hear himself repeating, repeating.

That night next to Ms Puss under clean marital sheets, the two of them alone in house, Oldcat watch a ghostly new moon float outside their window and wonder about Meow and Grrr at the lakeside cottage. They soon be getting married themselves—Grrr already as much as engaged to sweet girl named Michelle, keeping with M's after heartbreak over Melissa.

As moon float, Oldcat wonder if he will ever tell his grandchildren about the amazing second miracle of the multiplying loaves. Probably not, he decide: one miracle a lifetime is all we humans can bear. Let children and grandchildren experience their own.

The Girl with a Mountain Inside Her

Oldcat, innovative vice-president of HowYouSayIt Electronics, been demoted to go-fer at local grocery store because Ms Puss sick with springtime flu. Walking by vegetable aisle in store, him notice tall girl whose Mennonite white handkerchief barely detract from her long blonde hair, whose Mennonite blue-grey sack dress barely restrain her budding womanhood. He also notice, while handling hard green banana bunch— of all stupid thing—how this heightsome girl have wandering eyes for all the young men, and even—Oldcat surprised to note—even for himself.

Oldcat quickly drop bananas in cart. That bunch of hard lumps just as far as things going to go, cause he had enough wick-dipping for lifetime with Jackie Babe, and he damned sure not going to get involved with Mennonite teenager who have protective, crazy-bearded elders wielding chain saws and axes and hovering and poking around her angelic blonde hair all the time.

This local Mennonite community have good reputation in Carpenterville: you want odd-job hauling, carpentry, lawn work—they the people to call. And two Mennonites run the local hardware store that manages to stay in business despite Wal-Mart. In fact, a stolid Mennonite woman even rings up sales in Wal-Mart, her kerchief pressing tightly over her pinned grey hair lest scanning the bar code of a Madonna VCR corrupt her even more into the modern world.

Oldcat past the potatoes now, and smelling bread. Him remembering small 10-cent loaves of white bread that Rainbo Bakery make for children when he exist as a young thing in Kentucky. Ms Puss call white bread "white poison," and she probably right about that: just look at his own childhood.

With unsighed sigh, he reach for whole wheat and notice lanky Mennonite girl standing near cold cuts, her lanky legs cambering indecisive, like she a mare at county fair. The way she turn to look at him, though—she no cold cut. Good thing Alabama yet to pass stalker law or this girl be behind bars despite her fair teenaged sex and angelic hair.

Anyway, how old this girl, Oldcat wonder. Fourteen? Fifteen? Her so-much hair so much flaxen and beautiful that it like wild grape vine skimming through trees, bending gently to touch ground and offer sweetly bursting scuppernongs to Adam and other passersby.

Oldcat remember that the Mennonites pull their children from school in Alabama after tenth grade, arguing that children no need further education, no need further "English" ways. This girl have to be near tenth grade—what age that, fifteen, sixteen?

Oldcat push cart into drug aisle with deodorants, douches, anus ointment, headache powders, prophylactics, lubricating jellies, and foot-odor eaters—all landsliding from shelves in potlatch of Americana. Him stop cold and stare: yes, this be America. *Yes, yes, you Mennonite elders. Hurry and remove your innocent girl from school before she and her wandering blue eyes inundated in brown American muck like swank, landsliding California home. What disaster insurance ever cover that?*

Oldcat spot girl two more time while he shop, and each time she sly-spying at some male in the store, wondering maybe if—well, keep it clean, Oldcat tell himself—wondering maybe if Englisher boys kiss differently than Mennonite boys.

Last time he see her, she by animal supplies, which in this rural grocery store include rabbit pellets, horse feed, and chicken scratch. She so hot staring at boy down the aisle that Oldcat fear nearby grains going to spontaneous-combust into flames. Yes indeed, this girl-woman birthing volcanic mountain inside her, undulating deep lava flows in her thighs and recesses. What she have, in essence, Oldcat realize while settling smoke-flavored dog bones in shopping cart, what she have is mountain enough to move any faith.

Sundays

Smoke Gets in His Eyes

The Fall after Grrr and Meow gradualate from local Catholic high school, Ms Puss begin nursing-degree program while they begin U of Alabama. *Her* second semester, she learn that medical doctors inject laboratory rats with hormones to mimic Alzheimer's Disease in humans. *Their* second semester they learn that Jim Beam make whiskey; Budweiser, beer.

"They young," Oldcat console as she sitting at breakfast room's hardwood table, already frustrated over coming exam while twins already calling home collect to ooh-ahh about three rush parties in one week.

"That right: they young, and us old rats have all contracted Alzheimer's. That's why we no can remember what vitamin cause blood to clot."

The telephone make sudden ring and Ms Puss angrily scatter nursing exam notes over kitchen table in a flurry reminiscent of the great snow storm of umpety-doo.

Oldcat, he know when to let a bee be, so he answer phone in the dining room and leave Ms Puss buzzing over upcoming anatomy and physiology exam. After solving call from HowYouSayIt supervisor about minor problem their youngest pup Ralph could have barked the answer to, Oldcat stroll outside to sit on deck and breathe open country air in imitation of favorite slender TV yoga teacher. But even outside, he can still hear Ms Puss inside muttering about "damned phones" and "why can't Ma Bell make them soundless *and* cordless."

Thank god, Oldcat think, that the call wasn't another collect-for-anyone panhellenic party update from one of the twins. Him yoga breathe and sip caffeinated coffee—the two contraindicative? he wonder, already picking up medical vocabulary from Ms Puss. Too bad he can no remember what vitamin causes blood to clot, and thereby help her out.

Of sudden, maybe cause of an early morning shiver, he remember the time him sitting at amphitheater at University of Kentucky. He very young then—seven, eight, nine—and went with babysitter to outdoor movie to watch *The King and I.* A silly bald man with greased lips breaking out in song on mosquito-y screen below is all he remember of film beside mostly hard, cold concrete abutting his own tiny butt. Oh yes, him do also remember more technicolor than he ever thought possible in God's entire world revolving far on screen below. Impressionable him-child must have thought: It so brilliant and real down there on that screen, while up here, this concrete cold so dull and dark. It a flashing wonder he never want to be a movie star.

Now he scootch warm, old-fogy electronic engineer butt on sunlit cedar bench and drink hot, uni-color black coffee. But bango! Next minute, he remember being taken to funeral of neighbor who drowned fishing. "See how alive he looks, Oldcat? Go ahead and touch him," neighbor's fresh widow urge. Oldcat do touch dead flesh and pull back, though all he really care to do is cry, cause this man act as him second father when Civil War buff dad get too busy collecting dead lead bullets, which often more than often enough.

A blackbird one hundred yards in front of Oldcat's own cedar picnic perch skims the ground like a running squirrel, like it's forgetting what species it exist to be. Oldcat watch it, then realize that yoga meditation not working so very well . . . maybe he been thinking too much of how pretty instructor is.

Of another sudden him remember being in a woods with two child friends when one shoot other in forehead with a BB gun and both tangle over black log in big fist fight, which a frightened Oldcat try to stop by hopping on log like he too a squirrel searching for a nut. Of course fight end with them being best of friends, with Oldcat being crazed squirrel or forgotten acorn.

Oldcat breathe extra deep and stare at coffee mug, his clenched hand shaking from so many memories arcing through his synapses so fast. There a vitamin making him do that? Coffee, it leaching C, right, but maybe it promoting some ancient yoga essence just like what pretzelling through pretty insructor.

As if to prove fact, after next sip him of sudden flashing to lungs bursting full of happy, hot and humid Gainesville air after running the tiny warm football past eleven maroon and gold Florida State jerseys. Crowd's cheers physically shiver Oldcat's helmet, just like the whole stadium alive and broiling in his skull. . . .

Sportball.

He always put himself on hard-braking automatic stop whenever the subject of his football past emerge—what good it do to remember all that, beside make him spine hurt? For Oldcat know that unlucky seven plays later that him back . . . STOP! he shout at self and yoga breathe.

But yet one more college memory intrudes as he suddenly pictures girlfriend Sue who got hooked on pot or his or her own misfortune, one or all. Before pot, her eyes dove so deep a brown that they resembled Lady Godiva chocolate. Then him million dollar halfback back got hurt and things all mixed together, turned mudpie stupid—her eyes and sports memories both. . . . He guess that's because whiskey got in his belly, marijuana got in her eyes. Ha, smoke get in her eyes. That just like moldy oldie Platter's tune, yes?

But Oldcat not really laugh. Sometimes he miss Sue, sometimes he imagine that she's right down the block playing her Simon and Garfunkel record, putting on frosty make-up and waiting to drive with him to an all night frat-jock party.

Across the small rise one field away, say a hundred yards, a stag deer trots out, looks at Oldcat and his house, then trots on. Those distant antlers show so elegant, show so sure of themselves prancing along, that Oldcat want to sprint after them and squish leafy soil between his toes and up to his high arch, want to grip a pigskin in his hand, want to hear crowd cheering and stomping in stands, want to lie down with Sue in Payne's Prairie outside Gainesville where they first make love, want to forget HowYouSayIt Electronics, forget the twin's college bills from University of Alabama, forget middle-aged, uptight nursing student wife, skitter on legs and forget even what species he exist to be until . . .

With surprise, Oldcat remember to yoga-breathe. In with good air, out with bad air. Why all this memory junk smokescreening around today anyway?

Him stick mouth in coffee mug and quietlike prayshout so no one except Who-Am/Who-Is can possibly hear: *Ms Puss! Ms Puss! Study hard, so hard! Become a nurse soon and sneak me weekend Alzheimer's injections from hospital. How is it that every lucky human rat been able so far to undergo one but me?*

The Mystical Apple

It years back that bachelors Oldcat and Tom take vacation trip to St. Augustine. "This city we're going to is the oldest city in America," Tom intone from the passenger seat of Oldcat's red Mustang, changing the topic from Oldcat's ever-present harangue about the lack of Summons County and Carpenterville bachelorettes to the topic of Florida, by reading a tourist brochure while sipping his beer. "The city's so old that it's named after a Roman Catholic church father. Ha. How d'you like them apples—a church father."

"Church father. That anything like a church mouse?" Oldcat ask, smacking him lip and wetting him whisker with a grin, reaching into the cooler between them for another beer to make him stupider than he already am, even though him driving.

Tom, he look sly at ex-football player friend. "I'm trying to develop your mind into something besides a rotting pigskin, Oldcat. You know that St. Augustine, he's the one who confessed that the idea of a stolen apple got to loom into a bigger sin dwelling in his mind than actually eating the damned thing in the first place."

Tom, though him only the supervisor of tv/radio cabinetry at Summons Electronics, he read more books than six English professors at a convention, and him no doubt a misplaced nuclear physics genius, Oldcat always been think. So no wonder then that Tom's present speech confuse Oldcat.

"You kidding me? How can a thought-apple be more better than a red apple?" Oldcat swerve car to avoid hitting an armadillo trundling across the highway in the early dawn. "Them Roman Catholics're something, huh?" Only thing Oldcat not add to top conversation is a belch.

Tom, he just grunt, remindful of armadillo snort in heavy grass.

My goodgod, surely Alabama Southerner Tom's not a Roman Catholic, Oldcat worry, since he only know Tom for four month. Then Oldcat remember the Roman Catholic Church St. Francis of Assisi sitting in southwest Carpenterville, and remember that it even have a small yellow brick school attached.

But Tom not really seem to mind Oldcat's comment, he just continue explaining concept of thought-apple-sin, so Oldcat try his hardest to listen, though some Devil force him to keep envisioning blue and orange bikinis and not fruit.

Once arrived at city of St. Augustine, they check-in to motel, sleep three hour from all-night trip, get up, drink lunch, act like young foolcats that they are: worship sun, play frisbee, kick sand into pretend sandman weakling's face for benefit of two onlooking young ooh-la-la's garbed in handsome pink and yellow bikinis.

Oldcat show himself choosy about decorator colors: "Me take yellow, you take pink?" he asks Tom as seagulls scree overhead.

Ahh, but the quickest laid plans of seagulls and men may gong away, for pink bikini lady, she the one and only indubitable Ms Puss, you see. Yes, it true: Oldcat have to drive all the way to Florida to meet bachelorette living just one Alabama county, over just one Alabama river away from Carpenterville.

After five Florida hours, Oldcat plunge into Lake of Love. For proof of dunking, him pee more times that afternoon than he have in week, though him hardly even bothering to drink ice chest of beer him and friend Tom stow aside.

Next morning, Ms Puss and Oldcat slip quietlike away from friends Tom and Jackie Babe (this Tom's automatic nickname for varoom-acting Jackie, and she accept it like it an engagement ring). After small cup of Cuban coffee in local cafe and much daylight astronomical gazing into star-crossed eyes, Ms Puss and Oldcat decide to improve minds, visit St. Augustine's museum.

In that quaint brick building, they are bombarded not only by leftover Cuban sugar and caffeine, but by Winston the Churchill's stuffed lion, by ancient musical instruments that resemble gold-flaked cereal boxes, by two enclosed glass cases of dirty silk hankies the museum's director must have promised some grandmomma to display as eternal keepsakes upon receiving major endowment in will, by three wall displays of broken china that no doubt from ditto grandmomma's hope chest, by swords and hatchets galore, by one genuine mummy, and by two free-standing, shiny suits of armor.

Ms Puss peek into visor of second suit and call out, "Hello, my shining knight, you in there?"

"This silliest place me ever enter," young Oldcat announce to equally young Ms Puss, pulling her off armor before guard come around.

Silly? Of course, it only youth that make them agree about that judgment of silly, for if they stop star-gazing and glance at the surrounding world, they see for sure fact: Anyone ever want silly, societies from the globb-ular globe we live on offer plenty example, not even need to nudge into topsoil.

On museum's second floor, Oldcat have to go pee, not because of Cuban coffee like him claim, but because his ever-deepening dunk into lake of love keep him hormones squirting overtime. After flushing and double-checking zipped pants (This no time for Freudian un-zip slip!), he return.

Ms Puss smile, he smile. This realism or what, they think. Then they spy, outside multi-paned lead window, friend Tom and Jackie Babe on hobbled street below, walking hand-in-hand to talk. Ah life, ah stars, ah fortune. . . .

Back at motel room late that night, Oldcat pronounce to Tom: "Ms Puss, she the humdinger for me. I so in love that I think I . . ." him no can finish, for he have to go pee.

Next day bring beach 'n' fun, next night bring surf 'n' turf. Also bring enough beer, sand, and quiet walks around quaint little St. Augustine shoppes to infuse any living mammal with dreams of nesting.

"You ever," Oldcat hum to Tom as they change clothes to meet gals for dinner on the third night, "you ever think of marriage?"

Tom, he pop open a beer and look sly. "Remember what the namesake of this town taught? Remember what we were talking about just two days ago when we drove in? About that thought-apple?" This Tom's only reply while Oldcat in bathroom once more making water.

"What in the world does that mean?" Oldcat ask, walking out of bathroom. "Hurry up and get dressed or we'll be late."

"We early, they wait. Besides, you going to zip up, or just let it hang out?"

Oldcat look down and frown. . . .

Walking by a white sports car with an Alabama tag near gals' motel room, Tom, he spy *Bride* magazine lying in front seat. He yank at Oldcat's elbow, show him the magazine, and shake warning finger in Oldcat's face. "See what I mean about St. Augustine and the thought-apple? She looking hard, just like you. Still, you both need to sample Delicious, Macintosh, Winesap, Rome, Granny Smith, even crab—as many as you can before you take final bite."

Oldcat only make a pfft noise for a reply, sounding like his zipper, oiled with suntan lotion, quietly wiggling its way down to save his fingers fumble-time in the torrid Florida heat.

Once they inside gal's air-conditioned room, Tom ask, "That white sports car out there, is that yours?"

"It mine," Ms Puss reply. "Why?"

"It's nifty, that's all." He try to catch Oldcat's attention, but that like trying to steal an apple from tomato vine, so Tom's face just contort in a half smile, half sigh.

. . . Six months later, it come about in Carpenterville that Oldcat and Ms Puss wed. Tom best man; Jackie Babe, she the maid of honor. Tom give them wedding present of *St. Augustine's Confessions,* complete with fake holy relic autograph all swirled with following pig Latin inscription: "*Ad Oldcat et Ms Puss: Rex et Regina of Pommes Mystica.*"

"Oh, St. Augustine, that where we met," bride and groom explain book's title to onlooking wedding guests. Everyone read the inscription again and now think it funny.

"What are Pommes Mystica?" Jackie Babe ask.

Tom, he just take pretend bite of pretend apple and look sly. His two friends Oldcat and Ms Puss immediately give off big, assured ho-ho, cause *they* have nothing to learn from orchard and moldy-dead church father St. Augus—oh no.

Horizon

How many pale ice maidens Oldcat been in love with? He count out one day. First, girl at UK when he visiting campus and being wooed by Coach Fran Curci and football team. Yes, but when she smile at big hunk him, he can only return terrible face because viney coliseum nearly fall down it so old compared to SEC others and because winter-cold British sports car won't start on top of that. Poof! She gone from his love-dream like good cider squished from bad apple to be sold uptown.

That okay, if he fail in Kentucky hometown, he soon to be U of Florida football star, so other fatal femmes bat their eyes, don't no worry. What about boat girl, huh? Slush-slush, she float in mysterium circlestances on houseboat in South Daytona Harbor and wear ringlets in her chestnut hair like Christmas Day, 3 A.D. To her, though, football hero Oldcat more like a gobbling Thanksgiving Turkey than pigskin star, so once her bedtime snack finished, him carcass no doubt start to stink, a football left too long in hot local swamp. "Bon Boy-age," she shout, heaving him off gangplank into South Daytona drink.

Hey, man, that okay: there emerge other ice maidens from memory freezer; don't give up. Pretty Ft. Lauderdale reporter soft shoe along with feet so beautiful they probably type all her lead stories. But this reporter, she not only good at English, she excel at math: "Sorry, Oldcat, but quit your panting and windsprint back to Gainesville's artificial turf: your one and my one never to two will sum."

That all? No way, plenty more ice maidens come. What about ballet girl who work with Oldcat on his broked back? Hoobadooba, she have black hair prettier than Death and her frame so ballet-tight that it speak French and one other living foreign language. But mentioning death, her daddy die before Oldcat even know Cupid's arrow had him in butt struck and she depart University of Florida forever. Once more, Oldcat a Temple orange left miserable out in frost. Moresomeover, despite ballet and yoga, him back remain same as before: broked all up, able to play football no more.

Fie on thee Capitol C, for both Corrupting Cupid and Crummying Chance!

And then, of course, there brown-eye Sue. . . .

Ahh Oldcat! INITIAL QUESTION: Why you doing all this think-worry anyway? Why this ice maiden stuff howling like sudden blizzard? You planning Arctic vacation? You unhappy with Ms Puss?

Not-not. Not that. Me in Paradise with Ms Puss. But when in subtropical paradise, each far-off ice maiden gleam like crisp northern apple, despite though if living in Norway that same apple get frozed and on consequent those same ice-maiden breasts and toes beri-beri all winter long and come spring thaw stink like rancid jalapeno from hell. They in effect be just like stupid British sports car that never start in cold.

So, FINAL ANSWER: No. There no big problem at home. I just ongoing existence as-like any typical ungrateful human savage—always climbing the incidental tree to peer over the horizon. That all.

Even Love

Oldcat and Ms Puss once wake to blue countryside sky outside new house window, then both look into one another's astonished eye.

"Me have dream," both say, breathless.

Laugh at that, they do.

"Well, what yours?" both ask.

Ahh, synchronicity prove they in love finally and for true: this clear now, despite what misadventure happen two year's ago Labor Day between Oldcat and Ms Puss' once-best friend, Jackie Babe.

"Well, you tell yours first," both say.

Oldcat, ever since football days, never been much gentleman except in his heart, so him rush to explain his dream: "I was standing inside a grey stone hall. Sunlight come in one end—I remember seeing golden dust floating in the sunlight—but the other end behind me was dark. You know who walked in then? My friend Ray who's been in the Navy. I ever tell you about him? We've known each other so long that hair's grown between our ears. I see him sit down at a stone bench in this hall—Ray's a wood sculptor and artist. I see him carve out a woodblock that looks like a silent Mexican god, half frown, half grin. Tap, tap, tap—I even hear his chisel in my dream—and the wooden god opens its mouth to dribble black oozing oil from its snake tongue—then the chisel slips and Ray slices off his finger. But you know what?"

Ms Puss, she look too shocked to answer, but Oldcat ploddle on: "When Ray cut his finger, I felt the pain and yelled. He just lay lumped on the granite floor, blood thrumping from his hand."

Bright morning light shine through new Wal-Mart sheer curtains. Ms Puss blink and grab her husband's hand, scratch his leg on accident with her big toe because they still in bed. "Oldcat, I'm scared. I had nearly the same dream, except with my friend Sheri from high school. She owns a bakery now, but in my dream she stood under a shed near a dirty brick kiln baking evil-looking loaves like those three grey gargoyles Meow left in her bedroom. She put a trayful of these in her kiln, and one gargoyle loaf rose over all the others and opened a black, cavernous mouth. She jumped away and burned her hand on the kiln door so badly that she fell and hit her head on a wooden post. The bread gargoyles all dripped dried black blood from the open oven racks. I awoke with scream and—" Ms Puss hold up own hand, almost willing it to be burned pink in a stigmata.

They stare at the window curtain until a breeze lifts it. They both so weirded from synchronous dreams that they dress and drive to Madame Walter, famous Christian Reader down the road.

Dark-skinned gypsy-looking son out in yard mowing as they pull up. Him stop mower and nod toward house, yelling, "Mom!"

From mini-van, Oldcat and Ms Puss study large tattoo on son's arm. They both move last spring from Carpenterville to country to get away from city evil-lookers, and now here trot one in the country killing innocent green grass.

Madam Walker appear sudden in door, her black hair swirled with striking gray, through it all together stacked to the lintel. It obvious that she's a Dixie gypsy. Maybe even, she use grits instead of tea leaves.

"Why . . . our new neighbors," she say. "Welcome." Her large-framed body open her door.

Inside, her house smell like something Oldcat cannot . . . yes, that's it: incense. Crucifixes debris many of the blue walls, alongside glowing pictures of Jesus. Just as Madame Walter a Dixie gypsy, she a Christian psychic—only kind of either that Alabama likely to tolerate.

"We both had a dream," Ms Puss timidly say after they sit at table and drink coffee.

"Ah," Madame Walter respond, straightening like the upright beam to Calvary's cross.

"It wasn't the same dream, but then it was." Oldcat adds.

"Ah," Madame Walter respond, and her eyes grow wide and she gaze to crucifix on nearby wall, motioning with her red, dish-soaped left hand for them to continue while naked, bloody Jesus solemnly climb down from the cross to enter her soul and guide her.

So they both tell dreams. Then Madame Walter speak, rubbing finger along patch of gray hair:

"You two have a mutual friend who needs you very much. Go to your friend right away, before it's too late."

"Too late?"

"Too late. Your friend is very sad."

"Sad? Is it a relative?" Ms Puss ask, thinking of her mother, her sister.

"That I cannot tell. The currents are too weak. Hurry, though. You must hurry."

Oldcat and Ms Puss try to pay, but Madame Walker tell them they neighbors. "Hurry!" she insist.

So they leave, drive along country road, avoiding the one name they both know to know. Finally, Ms Puss dare say it: ". . . Jackie?"

Oldcat swallow spittle at poison topic. "This what we get for going to a palm reader in the first place—"

"She no read our palms, Oldcat. She interpret our dreams."

Oldcat shrug, as if to say same-o, same-o, no?

"Drive to Jackie's, right now!"

"But—"

"Drive, Oldcat, drive! Hurry!"

Oldcat speed, running six-seven rural stop signs and not even waving at cows, chickens or stray dogs. Once in Carpenterville and parked, Ms Puss turn into a crazed woman: she bang-bang on Jackie's door, then break a back window while Oldcat, wide-eyed, imagine police blue lights, newspaper headlines, etc.

"Oldcat! Get in here! Call 911 and tell them to send an ambulance! Jackie's slashed her wrists!"

Oldcat run into bedroom where Jackie lie in bloody sheets.

"She's alive," Ms Puss say, stroking Jackie's blonde hair catching her finger in a ringlet.

Jackie wake enough to look at Oldcat and groan.

"This is impossible. Life doesn't happen like this."

"Oldcat! Did you call 911?" Ms Puss turn with razor blade in hand, and for single moment, Oldcat afraid she going to cut her own wrists or his. But she drop razor on bed stand with tingle like a bell, then turn to Jackie, who dry-retch and cough, then groan.

Oldcat run to kitchen. 911 such a simple number, he realize as he dial. And life, it pose such a ten million piece jigsaw puzzle: *Affairs with best friends, psychic readings come true, bloody crucifixes with still-living miniature gods, suicide attempts, buzzing summer flies—anything possible in piecing jigsaw together. Sunny afternoons, ambulance sirens, psychic powers, forgiveness . . .*

"911. Hello? Hello?"

"Hurry," Oldcat explain. "314 Walnut Street. She's tried to kill herself. Hurry."

. . . stray dogs howling in nearby field, coyotes in the Alabama night, cool summer gin and tonics, friends arguing and making up, parked trucks bouncing on a moonlit Labor Day dirt road, betrayal, forgiveness—even love.

"Hurry," Oldcat tell telephone receiver and humming electric clock over Jackie's dirty yellow stove. "Hurry, for love."

Mystery Tonight!

Ms Puss, being neonatal unit nurse for one year, going to attend her first nursing conference.

"I no sexist pig like you, Oldcat. I take my spouse along."

"I just always thought that you would have been bored at—"

"Oldcat, Oldcat. Your tongue growing longer than your arms from lying. Better hush or you soon be wearing Ace bandage on it."

So they drive to "Surfactant Therapy for the Neonatal" in Gulf Shores, Alabama.

"What this Surfactant Thing, anyway?" Oldcat ask.

"Surfactant's a lubricant for the lungs; it makes them pliable and able to breathe. Some premature babies are born without it, so doctors and nurses pump it in so the baby won't suffocate."

They silent for a minute, thinking about Michelle's baby, who never even have a chance to breathe. "You can do that?" Oldcat asks, amazed.

They drive past tractor outlets, flea markets, bars, miniature golfs, and huge outlet mall, into semi-redneck riviera of Gulf Shores.

"Yes," Ms Puss whisper, thinking of Grrr and Michelle.

Registration, coffee and donuts, and first meeting not until next morning. So relaxing in evening, Oldcat squish sand between toes and tell Ms Puss incident about strange wino with thirteen pocket overcoat stuffed with bottles, paper scraps, and cans, and how wino salute him on street at a conference in Washington, D.C. "Then all he do when I salute back is say, 'That's six! Great! That's six.'"

He dare Ms Puss to top that story after her conference tomorrow.

They just sitting at shoreside Pink Pony Pub before loud kid music start, hoping to have enough time to enjoy their seafood gumbo, a drink, the beach, and to watch the Gulf waters slurp up the helpless setting sun.

"Double relaxing," Ms Puss say, popping her neck and listening to waves while drinking wine.

"Triple relaxing cause I'm here with you," Oldcat rejoin.

Oh Oldcat, he turn into some romancer after Jackie Babe affair. Maybe mostly guilt at first, but him been smooth-talking so long that it become natural and sincere, like Pascal's Wager that Tom always talk about with great agnostic interest.

Ms Puss lean and touch Oldcat's shoulder as they watch college students bat volleyball and sand, back and forth. "Surfactant therapy," Oldcat chant as waves roll, making him feel like he been puffed with healthy new elastic lungs.

Next morning, he sitting alone on motel's balcony reading book friend Tom loan him called *The Mystery of Edwin Drood.*

—It's not finished, Tom warn when he loan it.

—What you mean? Oldcat ask.

—I mean it's not finished. Charles Dickens died before he finished it. Maybe when I retire from HowYouSayIt, I'll finish it.

—But then you'll ruin the mystery, Oldcat respond.

—Now you're catching on, Oldcat. I knew there was a reason they promoted you over me.

Tom right, too, about mystery book. It so misty creepy that Oldcat get chills even in brightly sanded sunlight.

At two o'clock, Ms Puss still at conference, so he put book down to walk beach. Girls, girls, pretty girls everywhere turning their bodies into temples of skin cancer, he suppose. Sun blast hot after forty minutes, so he stop for beer, have to be satisfied with Diet Coke because of state blue laws. Alabama must be only state in Union could screw up a beach—or maybe, on reconsider, it the only state in the Union can appreciate nature without drugs, who know?

Girls, girls, more girls in pastel bikinis, but they all so young now—even younger than his own daughter, who soon to be lawyer and probably second woman governor of Alabama. Who know? Maybe she even fix Alabama schools so children learn something beside racism, football plays and cheers.

Ah stop bittermoaning, Oldcat. This a vacation, not primitive Baptist Bible Study.

Oldcat listen to self and walk on to pass the state buildings where he know Ms Puss is meeting: its large patio empty except for six, seven people and Oldcat smile. Ms Puss taking meeting serious; she happy to have job, new life of own. Surfactant therapy. Yes, this nursing degree been a good thing for both of them. Oldcat's toes go hot as he pass a huge turtle sand sculpture. Who in the world would ever think of doing that? he wonder. Turtle's sand neck somehow supported—maybe they stick wire mesh inside—and turtle grinning like it going to pose him a riddle before he can pass. *What earth creature dringle on four legs in the morning . . .*

Oldcat obediently wait, but no question forthcome, so he walk on. After removing shoes and wading one more mile, the beach bums are taken over by sea oats, and the sun overhead is bearing down so hard that Oldcat lose all morning chill from *The Mystery of Edwin Drood. More like Mystery of Oldcat's Droop*, him think, wiping sweat from every possible face crevasse. So he turn around, trek back through girls, girls, girls; sip another Diet Coke; then decide to brave Jaws and wade farther out into Gulf and float, imagining self a dead Edwin Drood bobbing in Thames River. There the London Bridge. There the Tower of London. There a merchant ship laden with tea and spice. And there, isn't that my uncle Jasper motioning me to float ashore so he can resuscitate me?

It not Uncle Jasper, it Ms Puss in her hot-to-trot black bathing suit, waving arms like she a frisbee-playing coed.

"I did it! I did it!" she cry as Oldcat slosh from water, shaking off sea crabs and barnacles attached to his corpse.

"Did what?"

"I topped your sixteen-pocket-salute story. You aren't going to believe who I saw during a break today."

"Who?"

"Guess."

"The King of Siam. Charles Dickens. The inventor of surfactant therapy. President Clinton and First Lady Bill. Who? And how was the conference?"

Ms Puss tiptoe to give Oldcat a kiss. "Great. And all your guesses are wrong. I saw the turtle couple."

"The turtle couple?"

"Remember the time we went to a party when we first met and I was in JC? The party that wasn't really a party, but was at the Villa Apartments with the girl in my class and her submarine husband?"

"You saw them? You're kidding." A terrible feeling blister Oldcat: they been invited to another "party" and whole vacation on consequent ruined.

"Yes, but I was up on the elevated patio and didn't say anything. Guess what, though? They have a child, a little girl. And guess what they were making on the beach instead of a sand castle?"

The turtle. It dawn on Oldcat, but he hold back, wanting all of surprise to be Ms Puss's.

"A turtle! Of course, they were making a huge turtle right under where we stood. That's what attracted our attention in the first place. Don't you see? It's an omen, Oldcat, a good omen. Right after we saw them the first time you asked me to marry you. So now I know that Michelle's going to be all right with her baby."

Oldcat blink and breathe in. This been a subject no one in family broach, cause of what happen to Michelle last time on birthing table. But Ms Puss convince daughter-in-law Michelle and son Grrr to try again and change doctor, since she hear rumors about the one they have last time, and working with him as a nurse convince her sure they all true. Oldcat feel giddy in head, maybe from beers he didn't have and too much nature.

"Ms Puss," he say. "What is it that go on four foots in morning and . . ."

"And?"

"I forget."

"A turtle!" she yell running toward water.

So, soon both of them floating in warm water, returning to the womb and Thames River—replenishing their surfactant?

"We going to Pink Pony again for sunset?"

Ms Puss's voice startle him.

"What were you thinking of, Oldcat?"

"Putting a four-footed turtle in my retirement scrapbook. I'm saving all these clues to life as we stumble on them. I'm going to write a mystery to end all mysteries."

Ms Puss splash water at him.

"What about this evening? Can you solve that mystery? Are we going to watch the sunset from the Pink Pony Pub?"

Oldcat just smile a Buddha smile and refuse to answer. . . . Life, it be the best unfinished book there is.

Apropos

Oldcat and Ms Puss out walking with dogs, enjoying pleasant breeze, cracking of dried leaves, and musk of warming land promising one more spring. They've lived on this land just under one year now and things are swinging upward with twins leaving nest and Oldcat moving away from sin-town; but swinging downward with Senior Grrr getting in trouble at illegal University of Alabama fraternity hazing and with Jackie Babe trying to kill self over Labor Day affair and not blaming Oldcat nor Ms Puss so much they naturally have to feel guilty.

But think of today! Both Oldcat and Ms Puss tell themselves as they sniff noses into air just like their recently acquired pack of dogs.

Reason they have so many dogs? In Summons County, Alabama, it evidently standard operating procedure to let all dogs run wild and never carry them to vet for parvo, heartworm, spaying or neutering. Oldcat and Ms Puss talking about this even as they walk, and they decide it to be part of poverty-stricken county's fatalism, which witch twist her unhappy self to masquerade as old-timey good-feel Christian religion.

"Just remember how much Jesus the Lord suffered on Calvary's cross, etc. etc. . . . ," Oldcat intone.

". . . so whatever slop along—twin lousy racist school system, twin lousy broke-down ambulances, single lousy hospital—it all be God's inscrutable will, etc. etc." Ms Puss echo.

"Besides, we have thirteen bars for your enjoyment, just like thirteen apostate apostles."

"Amen, amen," they end.

Ms Puss pull flavored dog bones from pocket and try to teach youngest stray pup to sit. He no do, so she feed him anyway.

"If God meant him to be smart, him would have borned him outside Alabama state line—that what Alabamian peoples say, so why not Alabamian dogs think the same? That Alabama's glossolalia anthem," Oldcat tell Ms Puss, forgetting that she a native of state. But he on angry roll now, so no stopping: "These people so fatalistic that they might as well erect stone altars to the three Fate Sisters Clotho, Lachesis and Atropos in place of traffic lights at all the crossroads. That be apropos."

As Oldcat feeling thus superior, they top crest and descend toward large pond in back of their property. Ms Puss notice something move in branch next to pond and point. Another stray puppy? No, it's a—

It *was* a coyote. Their dog pack just slaughter it, after less than ten seconds of pulling and tearing, like they being timed for wind sprints in Crimson Tide's backfield.

Oldcat stand stunned. He being so proud, so domesticated, so intellectual, so rational, and now look what happen. Ripped and dead coyote floating in scummed pond water—who can tell which bloody side up? Ms Puss nearby, nearly crying. They turn back and look at bare path beaten with Old South clay, they turn forward and look ahead to more of the same.

Amen, amen. The Summons County summons. Maybe before being so decisive and righteous about their neighbors, they both need to stop at next cow crosspath and burn sacrificial coyote to three Fate Sisters, Clotho, Lachesis, and Atropos.

Yes, maybe that really would be apropos.

A Lonesomeless Note

Oldcat, every Sunday morning since last birthday threaten him with forty-five magnum worth of years, give up Hank Williams and be instead listening to classical music. All bell wanging, many violins scrying, trembling trumpets cannoning. *What head, what head this thought up,* he always admire. And when seven month ago he hear the One and Only Itzhak Perlman play, he wish himself to become a lonesomeless note shifting eternal through moony and cold, nights and days.

If he ever exist like so, he would look down and bless Ms Puss and her mother—he would even bless Ms Puss's hunk-browed father. He would bless Grrr and Meow. And he would bless the little creature crawling in daughter-in-law Michelle's puss, for sure, for sure, for sure waiting to come out and shout its caterwaul like the rest.

He would look down and bless his Japanese boss, who still have trouble with R's and L's. He would look down and bless his bachelor friend Tom, who just get released from hospital with pancreatitis and even now probably at Brass Chimpanzee or Oysterhead Lounge drinking beer. He would look down and bless Carpenterville's nativity scene and the single snowflake bouncing in a high-up Southern air current, ready to fall to hell's oblivion. He would look down and bless funny people not sanctified enough to look like him and Ms Puss in their skin, their nose, their eye—also not bright enough to speak American like them but rattle ba-ba, like same people who eventually chumble down Rome. He, in great and pure mercy, would even look down and bless mathematician who form Pi into strange number warbling just outside sanity and three—Why this number so wretched and hard, young Oldcat always had asked when him a scrimbling student. But he no mind it now. Now he envision all them—numbers and people—lumping proletariat together, marching, marching while he, a lonesomeless note, tremble with semi-celestial joy.

O music, o music, Oldcat wail with twitch of tail at chortling pale moon, *be like Pi: never you end.*

About the Author

Joe Taylor spent his youth in Lexington and Bardstown, Kentucky. After going for an endurance record at the University of Kentucky, he attained a B.A. in philosophy. He then moved to West Palm Beach, chasing unrequited love and extending his natural youth into an unnatural length. While in West Palm Beach, it occurred to him that all his jobs thus far—pizza cook, waiter, concrete worker, book buyer, and garbage collector—had primarily involved carrying objects. With this insight, he earned a Ph.D. in creative writing at Florida State in considerably less time than it had taken to get the earlier B.A. He married while at Florida State and has since lived with his wife, Tricia, in Atlanta, Tampa, and Coatopa, Alabama. He likes Coatopa best because it has neither a television station nor a professional football team.

Taylor has published more than fifty stories in various literary magazines, including *The Virginia Quarterly Review, The Florida Review*, and *Tri-Quarterly*. He was a reader for Peachtree Press and an editor of Sun Dog Magazine and Swallow's Tale Press, and he now directs Livingston Press. He has taught at various colleges in the South, including Kennesaw University, St. Leo College, and Georgia State University. Presently, he teaches at the University of West Alabama (formerly Livingston University).

He writes daily, usually with one or more dogs nudging each elbow, which, he notes, accounts for any typos in his manuscripts.